USA TODAY B1
SKYE MACKINNON

BOOK ONE

DAUGHTER OF WINTER

WINTER PRINCESS

PERYTON PRESS

Cover by MiblArt

Formatting by Peryton Press

Published by Peryton Press

Skyemackinnon.com

Contents

For my mum,
who made me fall in love with books in the first place.

Map of Scotland

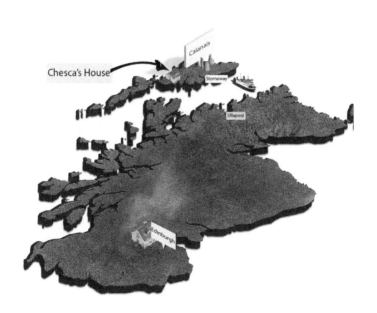

Glossary

This book has been written by a Scottish author using British English.

Here's a list of terms you may not be familiar with:

AA - people you call when your car breaks down (AAA in the US)
Aboot – about
Bonnet – engine hood
Calanais – also known as Callanish Standing Stones
Calling 999 – calling the emergency services (US: 911, Europe: 112)
Cannae (Scots) - can't
Cairn – a Celtic burial site/chamber
Dinnae ken (Scots) – don't know
Dreich (Scots) – bad, miserable weather
Flat – apartment
Having a fag – smoking a cigarette
Homely - homey

Glossary

Loch – lake
PS - horsepower (in a car)
RE - religious education (subject at school)
Tannoy - public announcement system (e.g. on a ferry)
Wee - small

Chapter One

If I told people that my mother was the Queen of Winter, they'd probably lock me up. And if I told them that I can do magic, they'd run away screaming. Or laugh, which is more likely.

It's not like I grew up in a palace or something. On the contrary, I grew up in a lacklustre semi-detached on the outskirts of Edinburgh, Scotland.

Nowadays, most people have never even heard of Beira, the Winter Queen. I'm not quite sure if I should feel offended about that on my mother's behalf. In the olden days, everyone knew her. She was known as the Mother of Gods and Goddesses, the Veiled One, the Cailleach, and, not very flatteringly, the old hag with one eye. You can probably guess which version my mother prefers.

Despite the legends, she certainly doesn't look like an old hag. Sure, she is old – and I mean, really old, even I don't know her age – but she is as beautiful as you can imagine.

Unfortunately, I didn't get those genes from her. I'm ordinary looking, nothing special. Dark hair, brown eyes and a few extra pounds around my hips that make me curse my jeans in the morning. I guess it makes it easier to blend in though. It's hard enough to hide my magic, so it's good that I don't have to hide unnatural beauty as well. Thinking positive, that's me.

My mum and dad are the only ones who know about my origins. They're not my real parents, of course, but they are a lot more paternal than my birth mother ever was. I've seen her exactly four times in my life. Five, if you count the moment I was born.

I get two letters each year; one for my birthday, one for winter solstice. She doesn't celebrate Christmas – Jesus and all that came long after she started her rule. I have 41 letters in my top drawer, every single one of them crumpled and stained from being read hundreds of times. Today, the forty-second arrived, in time for my twenty-second birthday tomorrow.

I've not opened it yet, but I've been holding it in my hands for the past hour, deciding whether it's better to open it quickly and be disappointed again, or wait for a bit longer, in the comfort of not being rejected - yet. Every time I get a letter, I write a reply, long and detailed, telling her about my life. Maybe it's because I want to make her feel guilty for having given me away. Now that I'm older, I understand her reasons, and I almost forgive her for it. Almost. If only she would allow me to visit her. In every letter, I ask. But I never get a reply. It hurts.

She doesn't want you. You're not worthy of being a goddess's daughter.

But now, I'm turning twenty-two. In Pagan tradition, I am coming of age. Tomorrow is the day my magic will specialise.

Winter Princess

At the moment, I can do basic stuff - light candles, levitate small things like books and cutlery (very handy when laying the table), open doors with my mind. Oh, and read emotions - not thoughts, although in most people I can deduce their thoughts from what they're feeling. I make a pretty good lie detector. It made me a pain for my teachers back at school, when I would call them out on made-up answers to pupils' difficult questions. Yes, I wasn't popular among teachers and my fellow students alike. Being able to see every fake or planted rumour for a lie takes the fun out of high school.

I'm not sure what will happen to my magic tomorrow. Usually, it changes, increasing one particular power and getting rid of all the others. That's why fire mages can't control water and so on. I've been thinking about it a lot: what power could I live without? Which one is my favourite? What kind of mage would I like to be?

But then, I'm not an ordinary mage. After all, my mother is a goddess. Which makes me a demi-goddess. Although I prefer to keep that one quiet.

There aren't many of us. To be honest, I don't know any other living demi-gods. All I have to go on are old tales and legends. None of which are particularly reliable. In most of the stories, demi-gods have a major power, but in contrast to ordinary mages, they also retain some minor powers. I really hope that's the case for me as well. I wouldn't want to go without my telekinesis. I haven't opened my curtains by hand in years.

I turn the letter in my hands. Already there are greasy spots on it. I should really get it over with. I'm used to her standard "PS. I'm afraid you won't be able to visit me this year" sentence at the end of the letter. The rest of it will be the same old: Happy birthday, let me know if you need any money, say hello to your adoptive parents. If I'm lucky, she might write a few sentences about her life – her life as a queen that is, not her personal life. I know next to nothing about my mother. The last time I saw her was five years ago, and even then, she only stayed for a day.

I sigh. There's no way around it. I slide my finger into the lash of the envelope and rip it open. The letter is folded several times and I open it apprehensively. The paper is thick and feels expensive. Guess as a queen you can afford nice stationary.

I scan the letter, skimming it for the all important words.

And there they are.

"Some of my most trusted guards will come and collect you on the evening of the 25th October. Please prepare to stay for a few weeks."

Wow. I almost want to scream in surprise and happiness. Finally, finally I'll get to see the Realms, see where my mother rules, find out more about – well, everything. Magic, gods, demons, and whatever other supernatural beings there are. I smile in relief. No rejection this time.

Then I read through it again. No further information. Besides a quick 'happy birthday' at the beginning of the letter, this is all. Typical. A few weeks... I'll need to clear that with my university. I'm doing a PhD, so I don't have classes I'd have to cancel, but I have assignments to mark for some of my professors. And after the autumn break I'll have seminars to teach - and now I've got exactly one day to sort it all out. Thanks, mother. You couldn't have told me before, could you.

I carefully put the letter back into the envelope and put it in my pocket. It'll join its brothers and sisters in my drawer soon. First, I have to talk to my parents.

Winter Princess

I climb down from my treehouse - yes, I'm almost 22 and I still spend time in the treehouse my dad built me when I was five - and knock on my parents' front door. We live in the same house, but the upper floor has been converted into a small flat for me. It's cheaper than renting my own place and I have privacy when I want it. Which is pretty much all the time.

My parents have always given me as much freedom as I wanted. Maybe that's because they're not my real parents, although they never made me feel like I wasn't their daughter. They would have likely done the same to their own children, if they had any. As long as I followed their main rules and got good grades, I was pretty much free to do what I wanted. Which usually ended up me practicing magic in the fields a few minutes' walk from the house (after I almost set fire to the living room once, this quickly became one of the unbreakable rules).

"Come in," my mum yells and I join her in the kitchen. She's making cupcakes - chocolate dough with chocolate filling and chocolate icing. Guess what my favourite food is.

I give her a kiss on the cheek. "They smell delicious." I try to steal one but she slaps my hand away.

"No cupcakes until we're all sitting down together."

"Mum, it's my birthday tomorrow."

"Exactly. Tomorrow. Now shoosh, get your father while I put the kettle on."

I find him in his office, staring at the computer screen. He looks tired and worn out. When did my dad get so old?

They were both in their forties when they adopted me. They wanted a child and when they were offered a baby girl, they accepted without hesitation. Even though they knew from the beginning that I was different. I love them for it.

I quietly knock against the doorframe. "Dad, tea is ready. Join us in the living room?"

"Aye, give me five minutes," he sighs, and turns back to his computer.

In dad-language, this means I'll have to come and get him in about ten minutes. At least by then the tea will be the temperature he likes: lukewarm, once you add milk.

I meet my mum in the living room and slump down on the sofa next to her. A large pot of tea is waiting on the little side table, as is a plate full of cupcakes. The next ten minutes are going to be torture. Can't dad be on time for once in his life? But then, I should know the answer to that by now. He's a bioethical researcher at the university, and when he gets started on reading a book or journal article, there's no stopping him. My mum is an artist, one of the few who actually manage to make a living from their paintings. She uses the shed in the garden as her studio, and often spends half the night in there. She's currently experimenting with fluorescent paints, which means it's easier for her to paint when it's dark rather than during the day. My bedroom looks out to the garden, and when I leave the window open in the summer, I can hear her hum from the distance. It's like she's singing me a lullaby without even knowing it.

"What are your plans for tomorrow?" she asks me and puts an arm around my shoulders. She's a very tactile person and gives the best hugs in the world. My dad is the opposite; he's more of a handshake guy.

"I'm going to meet Gina for tea in the afternoon, and we might head to the pub after. I was planning to do my birthday party on Sunday, but now..."

I notice I haven't told her yet. My birth mother is a bit of a sore topic in this house. I think my parents don't like to be reminded that they're not my biological parents. So I always make sure not to call her 'mother' in their presence.

"Beira has invited me to her place." That sentence sounds so ordinary. Except that 'her place' isn't on earth, and it's more of a palace than a house. At least, that's what she told me on her rare visits. I was five days old when I was brought to my parents, so I have no memory of the God Realms. I couldn't even tell you how to get there. All I know of the magical world is what I've read in the books Beira brought me on her visits. They are very basic, but at least they taught me how to do a few magic tricks. Everything else I learned through experimenting. Which, after I discovered I could make things explode, my parents made me do outside. Far away from anything that could break. Although I broke a tree once. Oops. I never told them that.

"Are you planning to go?" my mother asks, her voice a little unsure.

"I guess so." I try to appear more reluctant than I actually am. I don't want to hurt her by saying that I can't wait to explore the Realms, learn more about magic, find out which of the supernatural races human write about actually exist. (I was terribly disappointed when I discovered that werewolves aren't real. I always fancied meeting a hot wolf shifter one day.)

"She's sending some people to pick me up tomorrow. I might be gone for a few weeks."

"Oh. That's... sudden." She takes a long sip from her tea cup, hiding her face.

"I'm going to try and call if I can. I don't know if mobiles work over there, though. But I'm sure they have some way of communicating with this world, even if it's through letters."

"Thank you, sweetheart. I know you're an adult now, but with all this... magic stuff, I need to know you're ok."

"Everything will be fine, mum. Don't worry."

With a determined smile, she finishes her tea and gets up. "Come with me for a moment, there's something I want to show you."

I put down my own cup and follow her outside, through the garden and into her shed-studio. Large canvases line the walls and shelves packed with paints and other art supplies circle the room. This is the only chaotic room in my parents' house. Everywhere else it's tidy and spotless, but the studio is a manifestation of creative chaos.

My mum leads me to a cloth-covered easel. "I was planning to give you this tomorrow, but now... well, we don't know when they'll come and pick you up, so I thought I'd show you today."

She carefully lifts the white cloth (I'm sure it was a bed sheet once) and reveals a big painting on canvas.

I gasp. Then laugh. Then smile. Then almost cry. Then hug her.

When my emotions subside a little, I turn to take another look. A painted Wyn stares back at me. When you ignore that she's painted me in all colours of the rainbow, it's almost like looking into a mirror. My mum is a genius. But what's so special about the painting are the soft, intricate white lines that float around me. Magic. Even though she can't see it herself, she's painted them so realistic that they almost look like they'll jump out of the canvas to bring life to something spectacular.

"You haven't seen the best of it yet," my mum laughs and turns off the light. We're left in complete darkness – wait, not complete. As my eyes adjust, the painting transforms. My throat chokes up when I realise what she's done. The painted me has turned into a simple white outline on black while the magic tendrils are bright and colourful, exploding out of myself while at the same time hugging me gently.

"How did you...?" I am lost for words, which is not something that happens very often. I'll mark it in my calendar later on.

"Two years of experimenting," she says proudly. I can hear her move towards the light switch, but I tell her to leave it off for another moment or two.

Finally, I am no longer the only one who can see the magic. It's right there, on paper. It's like proof that it exists, that it is almost... normal.

Chapter Two

On birthdays, my parents usually wake me up together, with a cup of tea, a plate of pancakes and a candle.

It's been tradition for so long that when I wake up by myself, alone in my dark bedroom, it feels very wrong. I switch on my nightlight and look around. Everything is as it should be. No scary monsters under the bed (I hope, I didn't actually check). I look at my phone and sigh. It's five in the morning. Time to go back to sleep again.

"Happy Birthday, Wyn," I whisper to myself and switch off the light.

And gasp in shock.

My body convulses. Every muscle tightens and suddenly I'm in the foetal position, my limbs locked around my torso. White hot pains floods my mind, but I can't open my mouth to scream. I can feel my fingernails burying themselves in my palms and I know that I've drawn blood. My chest hurts and I can't breathe. I try to gulp up air, but my lungs refuse to obey.

I'm locked into myself, screaming inside, the pain threatening to drown me. Am I dying? Is this the end?

Without warning, my muscles relax, and with a rattling sound in my chest, I can breathe again. I take a deep breath, savouring the cool air flowing down into my lungs. My body hurts from the involuntary exertion. I lie on the bed, not moving, trying to calm down my breathing. What the hell was that? Was that some kind of physical illness or is it my magic going amok?

My throat is parched and I feel a little dizzy. I slowly get up and make my way through the dark flat until I reach my kitchenette. Pouring myself a glass of water and downing it in one go, I lean against the counter. My heart is still beating too fast. My hand holding the glass is shaking slightly. I am scared. Should I wake my parents? But then, maybe I'm overreacting. Maybe it's nothing.

Wrong.

I collapse to the floor, my body going limp. I'm not fainting, my mind is fully aware, but my body refuses to move. At least this time there's no pain. But I can't feel anything. No warmth, no cold, no tingling. Nothing. It's as if I'm completely separated from the body that's lying crumpled on the kitchen floor.

Then the clattering starts. It's coming from the kitchen cupboards: rattling, knocking, shattering. One of the cupboard doors above me flies open and out float four wine glasses, trundling in the air, gently knocking against each other with the most beautiful chime. They're followed by my mugs. Another cupboard opens. With a bang, a plate flies out and crashes against the wall opposite, breaking into a hundred pieces. More plates destroy themselves kamikaze style, and shards are raining down on me. I don't even know if they're cutting me; I still can't feel anything. The banging in my drawers gets louder until they fly open, releasing my cutlery into the air. The knives are flying around in a swarm, while the forks seem to be line dancing. This must be a dream. Only in a dream forks can dance.

There's a loud knock on my door, and I can hear my father shouting, but I can't respond. I'm trapped within my body, surrounded by flying crockery. The knocking turns into banging, and with a crash, the door flies open. A second later, my parents are standing at the kitchen door, wide-eyed and open-mouthed. It must be quite a sight.

"Wyn?" my mother asks, her voice trembling. "Why aren't you moving?"

Suddenly, the knife-flock turns in the air and assembles in something that looks like an attack formation, directed at my parents. My large bread knife spearheads its brothers. They tremble, then the first one shoots forward, aiming for my father's head.

NOOOOOO! I shout inside my head, and with a gigantic crash, they stop in mid-flight and fall down to the floor, together with the rest of my crockery. A plate hits the ground next to my face and a shard buries itself in my cheek. It hurts like hell, but it's a good pain, because I can finally feel again. I wiggle my fingers and slowly, they comply. But with movement comes the pain. I feel like I just survived a meteor shower. I am covered in scratches and my clothes are shredded by glass and porcelain shards. The one in my cheek seems to be the deepest wound though.

My parents are still standing in the doorway, staring at the carnage that was once my kitchen.

"Wyn?" my dad croaks. "What was that?"

"Are you alright?" mum whispers.

I just nod, not yet ready to speak. And I don't have any answers anyway. Usually, my telekinetic magic allows me to lift one plate at a time. If I concentrate really hard, I can lift two, but only for a few seconds at a time. This is crazy.

I slowly stumble to my feet, brushing the debris off my ruined clothes. My cupboards are empty, their contents now lying destroyed on the floor. The only thing left on the counter is the glass of water I drank from earlier.

My eyes fill with tears as I look at the destruction I wrought. I'd always known magic could be dangerous, but not like this. What if the knives hadn't stopped? What if my parents had been hurt, or worse?

Tears are running down my face, mixing with the blood trickling from the cut on my cheek. I look down and see that my shirt is already drenched in blood, both from my cheek and from other, smaller wounds.

A sob escapes me, and a second later, my mum takes me in her arms, holding me as I cry. She isn't asking any questions, and for that, I am unbelievably grateful. For now, I just want to be sad. Maybe a little self-pity will make this better.

But it's not over yet.

This time, it's a headache. But not any kind of headache. A burning, splitting, all-destroying headache.

I feel my knees wobble and just manage to whisper "Get away from me" to my parents. If another magic attack is happening, I don't want them anywhere near me. I almost killed my dad once already, and the sun hasn't even risen.

They step back and I gently fall to the ground. This time, my body remains under my control, but with the aching pain in my head, that doesn't matter. I squeeze my eyes shut, trying to keep all light away from my senses. I've had migraines before, but never this bad. My head is being ripped apart and there is nothing I can do to make it better.

"Wyn!" I hear from afar. "Wyn, you need to stop!"

I don't know what he means. I can't look, I can't hear anything, all I feel is the pain and the rushing of blood in my ears.

"Wyn, please, look, you need to stop it!"

Their voices are becoming more desperate but I'm lying on the ground, my entire being encased in agony. I can smell something, but my mind isn't aware enough to figure out what it is. My parents' voices are getting quieter until they disappear. I'm on my own, alone with the pain. A roaring has started all around me and the smell is getting more intense.

Burning. I can smell burning. With all I've got, I manage to open my eyes a little. The light almost makes me pass out. It's bright, too bright. It shouldn't be this bright in my flat. It takes me a moment to process what I'm seeing.

Fire.

Lots of fire.

Without warning, the pain disappears and my eyes fly open, my senses fully aware again. I am surrounded by a circle of flames; so high they're licking at the ceiling. Somehow the smoke of the fire is kept outside of the circle around me, otherwise I'd likely be unconscious already. I concentrate, the way I usually do when I try to make a flame appear. But all I can do is light a candle; I've never tried to extinguish it.

Stop, please stop, I beg in my mind, but nothing changes. If anything, the flames are getting stronger. My kitchen is no more and I through the haze, I can see how the fire has spread through the rest of my flat. I am surrounded by a sea of flames. Even if I knew how to leave this circle, I'd never make it out alive. I just hope my parents got out in time.

"Mum! Dad!" I shout, but the roaring of the flames swallows my cries. I step forward, hoping that the circle might follow me. Instead, I singe my fingers on the fire wall. Sucking on them, I try again to concentrate on the flames. *Stop. Extinguish. End.*

It's not working. The ceiling above me is creaking; soon it will collapse, burying me under it. At least fire moves upwards, so maybe it hasn't spread to my parent's flat below mine yet. Maybe the floor won't collapse. Maybe they'll still be able to live in this place once I'm gone, once I've burned it all and myself.

Sooty tears are streaming down my face. How could everything get so out of control? Did my birth mother know? Why didn't she warn me? Why didn't anyone warn me my magic could do this? Had I known, I'd spent the night somewhere else, in some remote field where I couldn't hurt anybody.

Even though I have no control over the fire, I can feel how it's draining the energy out of me. It's using my energy to fuel its hunger. My legs wobble but I stay standing. I don't want to die on the floor, pitifully lying there, awaiting my end. I'd rather stand and look death into the eye.

The circle around me is slowly becoming smaller. The fire walls are closing in on me. The heat is becoming unbearable and I can smell my hair burning.

I guess this is the end.

I prepare myself. Once, they burned witches at the stake. Now, I'm burning myself. My magic is killing me. Oh what irony.

I feel faint, but if I fall now, I will fall into the flames. Need to stay strong.

Voices in the distance.

Then, figures, four dark silhouettes walking through the fire, unharmed. The flames are avoiding them - all except for the fire wall around me. When they stand close to my fiery prison, I can see that they are all young men, larger than average, but their features are hidden behind the smoke.

One of them is saying something, but I can't hear him through the flames. I try to raise my hand to my ears to show him that I cannot understand him, but the fire has crept closer again and I burn my hand, screaming. He shouts again, and then they're walking around the fire column until they stand in a circle. Four men, in symmetry, like a compass.

I feel something in the air, like a soft, gentle breeze that strokes my cheek. Then something is ripped from me, and I pass out.

Darkness.

I t's cold when I wake up. I don't need to think long about what happened, it immediately rushes back into my mind. The fire, the flying cutlery, the heat, the fear, the pain. Everything out of control. Feeling helpless. Trapped. A tear runs down my face, too late to be of much significance.

"Hey, easy," a deep voice whispers. I look up, only to find four men staring down at me. And behind them, my parents.

Through their legs, I recognise my street. The sky is filled with dark grey smoke and I can still smell burning. Apparently, the fire didn't disappear when I passed out. It's still devouring the house I grew up in.

"How are you feeling?" the same guy asks and gently lays a hand on my forehead. He's kneeling next to me, his bright blue eyes examining me closely. They're ocean-blue with turquoise specks around the pupil. I've never seen eyes this vibrant before. Blond hair is a mess on his forehead; it looks like he just got out of bed, but this effect likely took him hours in front of the mirror. His face is perfectly symmetric, his skin flawless. I know immediately that he isn't human. He's not a mage either - mages look human on the outside, and even though some can change their looks with their magic, they'd never be able to look this perfect.

His warm hand disappears from my forehead and I shiver. It's strange how not long ago I was almost burned to death, and now I'm cold. My teeth are beginning to chatter and goose bumps are covering my skin.

"Careful, she's flaring again," another man says, and four pairs of feet step away from me. It's probably better that way. I hurt people. I almost killed my parents.

The cold is taking over my body. My breath is coming out in a soft cloud. I'm shivering, unable to control it. Something touches my cheek, and when I look up, I can see snowflakes raining down on me. There's a sort of milky bubble where they start, hiding the view of the sunny sky. It's like I'm in my own little microclimate. Fighting against the shivers, I roll to one side and sit up. The semi-translucent dome is taller than me and about twice as wide.

People are standing outside of it - the four men, my parents, and I can see some of our neighbours coming out of their houses. Sirens are ringing in the distance, but I am too cold to care. Ice flowers are forming on the bubble, slowly blocking out the view. It's like someone is building an igloo around me. My jaw is hurting from all the teeth chattering. I have lost all feeling in my hands and feet. The snow falling down on me is getting thicker, and harder. It's slowly turning into hail.

Suddenly, something bumps against the dome. Another hit, this time from the other side. Hands are pressed against the milky substance, four pairs of them. Just like with the fire column earlier, there's one in each direction. Four men, fighting against my magic.

The dome is quivering and thick gashes are appearing on its surface. With a high pitched crack, it collapses, covering me in icy shards and a heap of snow.

A burst of energy is drawn out of me and my legs buckle. Before my knees hit the ground, arms wrap around me and pull me up. They're warm, hot almost, and pull me against an even warmer body. I'm still shivering and lean into the warmth, rubbing against it in an effort to dispel the cold that is clouding my mind.

Someone clears his throat above me. I look up and jump back. I was pressed against a man I don't know, and he's laughing at me. Oops. But he was warm, that's my excuse. He pulled me against him. It wasn't my doing at all. I'm innocent.

Then why do I feel so ashamed? I rub my arms, missing the warmth of his body. The cold air makes way to a warm breeze that gently hugs me. I sigh contentedly and close my eyes, ignoring the stares I'm most likely getting. The warmth is feeling so good. If it wasn't air, I'd hug it back.

"How many flares has she been through?" A man's voice, unfamiliar.

"Flares?" my father asks.

"The ice was one, the fire another. Did anything else happen before that?"

"Oh yes, she destroyed her kitchen. Made things fly."

"Air, fire, ice. Shouldn't be many more then."

What? More of this stuff is going to happen to me? I can't go through this, not again. I'm exhausted and fainting once was enough. I just want to go back to bed, forget about all this and be normal. Not human normal, I'll never be that. Demi-god normal.

When I'm all warm again, the mild air around me disappears. I open my eyes. The four men are standing in a row, watching me. One of them, with long black hair and a black cloak - yes, a wizard kind of cloak - is lowering his arms. He's looking exhausted. Tendrils of magic are slowly pulling back into his hands, taking the warmth of the air with them.

Not every mage can see magic; in fact, I only know of two others.

I give him a small smile. "Thank you."

He nods and gives me a small bow. Not a smile though.

"Storm. At your service."

"Storm? Is that your name?" I ask, a little confused.

"Yes, is something wrong with that? Your name is Wynter, isn't it?" He gives me an annoyed look. Oops, I upset the guy who just helped me.

"Yeah," I mutter. Don't remind me. I know every Wynter-winter joke there is. "Sorry."

"He's playing with you, lass," the largest of them laughs. He must have giant blood in him. His hair is as ginger as it gets, and he is wearing - please believe me - a kilt. I mean, yes, I live in Scotland and people here wear kilts occasionally, but that's at weddings or festivals, and not in everyday life. A beautiful white sporran is hanging right over where his - anyways, he looks like a Scottish caricature. Except better looking. A lot better looking.

"I'm Arc. And over there are Frost and Crispin." He points to the other two guys who've been quiet so far. One of them is the blond man with the blue eyes. The other, Frost, is the spitting image of Storm: black hair that falls to his shoulders, dark brown eyes, tall. Kudos to the parents who named their twin sons Storm and Frost.

"Hello," Frost says, smiling at me. While his brother is gorgeous and serious, he's gorgeous and friendly. Dimples are adorning his cheeks. I shoot a quick glance at Storm. Nope, no dimples there. I guess this will be the way to tell them apart. And the fact that Frost is wearing normal clothes, not looking like someone straight out of Hogwarts.

My mother rips me out of my men-admiring thoughts. "Are you alright, sweetie? What happened?" She pushes past the four men and wraps me in her arms. She's a slender woman, but her grip is strong. "When Beira wrote that you were going to—"

"What? She wrote to you?" I interrupt her.

"Yes, a few weeks ago. She—"

"Why didn't you tell me?" Anger is rising up in me and I clench my fists. She knew! She knew and she didn't warn me. I could have prepared, I could have stayed away. I almost hurt her. I almost died. The house was burning. Anger is overtaking me, and suddenly I start shaking. And with me, the ground.

I can see the people around me fighting to stay upright, but I have no such problems. The ground is holding me up, stabilising me, giving me strength, while I do its bidding. It has wanted to move for so long and now it has finally found an outlet. I can feel the pain of the earth where houses are burrowing deep into its skin. They shouldn't be there. It's not right.

I raise my arms and gather as much of the earth's power as I can hold. And then I let it free. The ground shakes violently and deep cuts open up in the tarmac. I only half notice the screaming around me. I am strong, and I need to make things right. I point to one house, and it crumbles like a giant just stepped on it. Its walls collapse and roof tiles cover the rubble like sprinkles on a cake. It feels good. I adjust my stance on the trembling ground and draw more energy into myself. There is so much magic in the earth, so much power. It's been waiting for a long time for someone to use it. I point my arms to another house and it leans to one side, aching, shivering, until it collapses, burying half the garden under it. I laugh. It looks so pretty.

Something touches me and with a simple flick of my wrist, I repel them. I'm busy, no one will get in my way. Another touch, this time from the other side. Again, I move my hand to make them fly away, but before I can do so, my arms are captured and pressed to my side. The magic I had ready to flow to one side bursts out of me into the ground. This time, I don't stay on my feet. I fall, hitting my knees on the broken asphalt. Magic is still flowing out of me, shaking the earth. It hurts. The gentle embrace of magic turns into a white-hot stream that uses my body as its conduit. I'm just a tool for it. A channel. It betrayed me. I scream and beat my hands against the ground. With everything I've got, I expel all the magic within me.

The ground shakes one last time, then it stills. My vision goes black and I sink backwards, into the warm waiting arms of my guardians.

Chapter Three

"Good morning, princess!"

A cheery voice wakes me. I don't feel cheery. At all. There's a drummer in my head who's decided that my skull makes a lovely drum. Ouch.

"How are you feeling?"

I groan and open my eyes. It's the blonde guy, with the turquoise-blue eyes. He's sitting on the side of my very, very comfy bed. It's so comfy I shouldn't be allowed to leave it all day. Yes. I can't leave, I'm sorry. Now let me sleep.

Unfortunately, Crispin has other ideas. "Come on, we need to get going. We've got a long drive ahead of us."

I groan again and am very tempted to throw a pillow at him – but that would be too much work. I heave myself up and look around. We're in a bright, friendly room that looks slightly unlived in – a hotel, most likely. Crispin is already dressed, as immaculate as his hair is messy. I throw back the duvet – and with a shriek, pull it back over my body again. I'm in nothing but my bra and panties.

"Don't worry, I've seen it all before when I undressed you."

"Not helping."

"You've got nothing to hide, princess. Now come on, the others are waiting." He jumps off my bed. At the door, he turns back. "You've got five minutes, then I'm sending in Arc."

I keep clutching the duvet for another minute, just in case he or one of his friends return. Of course, I've been naked in front of guys before, but usually I knew them and had chosen to take off my clothes. Or chosen to let the guy take them off for me.

When I step out of the room, the four men are waiting for me. Arc is in a kilt again (a blue-green one this time; apparently, he's not loyal to one particular clan), Storm all in black with a high button shirt (but no cloak) and Frost in a *Winter is Coming* t-shirt. They're all as different as they come – even the twins have their own distinct looks. And Gods, are they all gorgeous. My hormones are fluttering excitedly. Down, girls, they are off limits. I don't even know them, and it's likely just a job for them. Bring the princess to the Winter Queen.

"Ready?" Storm asks, his voice a low grumble. Eww, someone didn't sleep well. Or maybe that's just his general attitude.

I nod and follow them out of the hotel. When we step outside, I realise we're still in Edinburgh. And that yesterday was a mess. I stop in my tracks, making Crispin bump into me. "What happened yesterday? You know, after- "

"After you levelled the street?" Frost laughs.

"Not funny," Storm grumbles. "Arc had to spend two hours changing your neighbours' memories."

"Wow, you can do that?" I stare at the ginger Scot. He shrugs uncomfortably. "Aye, I guess."

"Are my parents alright?"

"Yes, your mother had a slight graze on her arm, but I healed it, so don't worry," Crispin says from behind me.

"You can heal?"

"How do you think you're up and walking?" Storm says impatiently. "Can we have this conversation somewhere that isn't among humans?" He says it like being human is an insult. That reminds me, I don't even know what they are. My mother told me her guards would come and collect them, and I know that one can heal, one can change memories and one can manipulate the air's temperature. I've not seen Frost do anything magical, but I'm sure he has some kind of amazing magic, just like the others. I can't wait to find out if I can do some of what they can. I'd love to be able to heal.

Before I can ask any more questions, Storm leads us away from the busy streets until we come to a small rental car place. While he goes inside, the other guys are looking at the cars on display, their eyes wide and mouths salivating. Well, maybe not the second. Men. Give them something shiny to look at and they forget all about the woman in their company.

"Where are we going?" I ask them but don't get a reply. They're too busy examining cars. Tsss, apparently it doesn't matter that they're not human, they're just as easily distracted by a few PS. Ok, that Ferrari looks quite nice, but as long as it gets me where I want it to, I don't really care what car I drive.

Storm comes out, waving a set of keys. I thought he'd rent some kind of sports car, something sleek and expensive, but we stop in front of a large seven-seat people carrier.

"Seriously?" Arc asks him. Frost is bent over laughing.

"It was on offer," Storm grumbles.

"We've got access to the royal bank accounts. You'd think we could afford to rent something more... like a car."

"Maybe if you lost some weight we would all fit into a nice car," Storm smirks.

"Oi, it's all muscle!" Arc flexes his biceps and then lifts his kilt to give me a view of his thick leg muscles. Thanks, didn't need to see that. He's probably traditionalist enough to not wear anything beneath the kilt.

"Let's get going, we've got quite a long way ahead of us." Storm shoos us into the car, taking the driver's seat for himself. Frost joins his brother in the front, while Arc claims the back bench. I join Crispin on the seats in the middle.

"Where are we going?" I ask as we drive out of the rental place and along Edinburgh's busy streets.

"Calanais on the Isle of Lewis."

"The Western Isles? That's in the middle of nowhere. Why there?"

"The standing stones are the closest portal to the God Realms."

"So we're going to step through the stones like in Outlander?"

Four clueless men look at me. Guess that book hasn't made it into the Realm's libraries yet (do they have libraries there? Or computers? Will my Kindle work?) Actually...

"I need to go home first, pack my stuff."

Crispin cringes slightly. "How much do you remember of last night?"

"Nothing really after the ...ehm... earthquake."

Arc roars from behind me. "She's calling it an earthquake. That's so cute!"

"Shut it, Scottie," Crispin shouts over the laughter. "Wynter, there's not much left of your house. Your parents are staying at a hotel for now until they can be recompensed. They were both rather upset, so we decided- "

"You decided!" Frost interrupts.

"Yes, I decided to put them out of their misery- "

"You killed my parents?!" I shriek, launching myself at Crispin.

"What? No, I put them in a coma- "

I growl, trying to rip Crispin's head off his shoulders. Let him try to heal that, asshole. He's gripping my wrists, trying to keep my clawing hands away from his face while I fight against the seatbelt stopping my legs from kicking him.

"Stop it, Wyn," Storm's deep voice booms through the car, "what he's trying to say is that they're sleeping for a day or two to recover from the shock of seeing their daughter burn down their house."

That hurts. I sink back, leaving Crispin to lick his wounds (a few scratches on his face, nothing major).

"Are they... mad at me?" I ask in a small voice.

"They'll be ok, lassie," Arc says from behind me and puts a large hand on my shoulder. "You cannae forget, they're human, so it was all a wee bit too much for them."

"So it's all gone? The house?"

"Pretty much, aye. Some things may be salvageable from the ground floor. And the shed is intact, 's far as I could see."

"Thank the Gods," I sigh. "Mum would have been furious as hell if her paintings got destroyed."

"There is no hell," Frost remarks. I see what he is doing and follow the change of topic.

"Then where do bad people go after death?"

"The really bad ones are usually snatched up by demons just before they die, and are taken to the Demon Realms as servants. The ones that die are judged and then sent back to Earth."

"Why would they...? Seriously? Reincarnation?"

"Yes, guess you could call it that."

"So I could be reborn as an ant?"

"No, you're not bad and you only get reborn as a human so you can make amends."

"Clearly you don't know me yet," I snicker. "But who judges us?"

"That would be telling," Crispin says, his eyes twinkling.

"Come on, tell me," I plead, fluttering my eyelashes.

"He doesn't know," Frost interjects. "None of us do. And it's not something all that interesting to us anyway."

"Why not? Don't you want to know what happens to you in the afterlife?"

"Oh, she dinnae ken," Arc grumbles in his broadest Scottish.

"Well, then tell me!"

"We're immortal, lass."

"Oh. So you're not mages?"

"Nah, we're Guardians."

"I know you are, Bri- my mother told me she'd send her guards, but what species are you?"

"We're Guardians, with a capital G. One of the five races: Humans, Mages, Demons, Gods and Guardians."

"So, there's like a lot of you? A Guardian realm? Little baby Guardians? Do they look as good – I mean, cool. Great. You're Guardians. Ehm, how does that make you different from mages?"

"We're immortal," Storm sighs. I guess he doesn't like me asking questions. Which kind of makes me want to ask even more.

"And no, there aren't many of us," his brother elaborates. "We're created by the Gods to serve and protect them. Hence the name. We live in their realms, and no, there are no baby Guardians. We don't procreate like humans do—" he says it with a certain distaste "-we are created when we're needed."

"So, let me get my head around that. You're not born, you're never children, you start as adults?"

"Aye, makes it easier for everyone, no dirty nappies," Arc jokes. There's a certain strain in his voice though that makes me turn around to look at him.

"Then why do you sound Scottish?" The other three guys roar in laughter while Arc's already rosy face turns bright red.

"My creator wanted to go back to her roots... She thought she'd enjoy hearing a bit of Scots." His voice turns bitter. "But it made her melancholic so she sent me to Queen Beira instead."

"And I'm glad she did, mate," Crispin says, now serious. "We would have been lost without you yesterday."

We stay quiet for a while. We've finally left the city behind and are now driving through arable farmland. Fields are lining the road, with fat sheep staring at us dispassionately.

I can still feel yesterday's exhaustion in my body, and close my eyes sleepily. Just a little nap.

I'm swimming in the sea. Jellyfish are circling me, dancing with me, while a group of dolphins are watching. I am part of the sea and the sea is part of me. When I swim, the creatures of the water come to join me. When I need help, they are there. When I am lonely, the give me company. I am the sea's creation and water is my element. I am born to control the water – it lives through me. I dance a graceful pirouette with one of the dolphins, giggling as her brother shows off with an especially complicated jump –

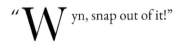

"Wyn, snap out of it!"

"Princess, you have to stop, you're – damn it, there's water in the engine, we have to..."

A slap against my cheek rips me from my dream. Crispin is staring at me, his shock mirroring my own. My feet are ankle-deep in water; the car is flooded. Oops. That wasn't planned. But then, so wasn't the earthquake and the attack of the cutlery. My magic is messing with me – it either wants to kill me or it's laughing in my face.

Storm is fighting a spluttering engine. Luckily, we are alone on this country road; I don't think other drivers would take kindly to his swerving.

"Pull over," Frost tells his brother. "Wyn, the water is still rising, would you mind making it stop?"

"Eh, sure." I concentrate really hard. Then, a moment later, I admit what an idiot I am. "How do I do that?"

"Are you serious?" Storm shouts. "I'm having trouble believing you're Queen Beira's daughter!"

"Well, she never bothered to come and teach me!" I shout back. A wave breaks over Storm's head. Oh oh, was that me? Sorry.

Crispin grips my hand. "You have to feel for your magic. What is it doing right now?"

I concentrate until I see the swirling magic tendrils around me, forming a thick white web on the bottom of the car. Water is seeping from it. I didn't know my magic could do that. There's some serious chemical stuff going on, converting air to water in a split second. I carefully pull back a few of the magic strands, destroying the net. With a tremble, it collapses in on itself and a cloud of steam bursts from within the car-lake. The water is still there, but at least it's no longer rising. I grin proudly, expecting to see some happy faces, but no such luck. Four stern guys are looking at me.

"Hey, at least I managed to stop it myself this time," I mumble, looking down at our wet feet. One of their phones is lying beneath the water's surface, another victim of my magic.

We get out of the car and wait while Frost calls the AA. At least it's nice and sunny, not your usual dreich Scottish weather. The guys are in a surly mood so I sit by myself, trying to make sense of what's happened in the past two days. It's crazy, there's no better word for it. I expected something to happen on my birthday, but not this. I didn't think I'd have so much power, and so little control.

I can see the sea in the distance, which means we've made it to the West coast, but I have no idea where we actually are.

"About ten miles from Oban," Crispin answers when I ask the question. He comes over and sits down on the grass by my side. "I'm sure there's a repair place there, so it shouldn't be too long a wait for the tow truck to come."

"Do you always drive to Calanais?"

He laughs. "No, we usually fly. Your mother owns a private plane that we can use. But with your powers being so unstable, we thought it would be a bad idea to be so far from the ground. Fire on a plane is never a good idea."

"How long will this magic thing go on for?"

"I haven't got a clue. I spent a few days in the Royal Library when we were given this mission, but there's pretty much no record of other demi-gods. A few human women claimed to have been impregnated by gods, but those children usually turned out to be human."

"What about the Greek and Roman demi-gods from the legends? Hercules?"

He laughs again, and I cross my arms and frown at him. It's not my fault I know next to nothing about my heritage. "Hercules was a mage who thought a lot of himself. He spent most of his money on scribes to write poems about his supposed strengths. You should ask your mother about him, she met him once."

"My mother met Hercules? That's kind of... weird." But I guess my mother has been around for long enough to have met all the important people in history. I don't even know how old she is. But they call her the Mother of Gods, so she must have been around since the beginning. I guess. My RE teacher never mentioned anyone besides the Christian God. I'll need to ask my mother about that one. "What about Zeus? Didn't he have other demi-god children?"

"Zeus is a lower God. He got some good PR in the past, but he's actually at the bottom of the hierarchy."

"So he's still alive?"

"Of course, what did you think? He's a God, they're immortal."

"Just like you Guardians?"

"Mostly." I raise an eyebrow until he expands on that statement. "We don't age and we don't get sick, but we can be killed. Decapitation is one of our enemies' favourite. Gods are even harder to kill."

"Who are your enemies?"

"You ask a lot of questions." I open my mouth to defend myself, but he smiles. "I like it. You only learn by asking questions. Our enemies are the enemies of the Gods. Demons, mostly, but sometimes a power-hungry mage decides to fight the Gods. Unsuccessfully, of course, but it's good practice for us." He gives me a grin that changes my perception of him from a healer to a warrior. I can imagine him in a fight (he's certainly got the muscles for it) and that grin says he'd enjoy it.

"If there are demons, are there angels as well?"

"The angels you read about in stories are usually Guardians. Most people don' know we exist, so when they see us, they give us names from their mythology. Angels, helpful spirits, prophets."

I'm almost embarrassed to ask the next question, but it comes out of my mouth before I can stop it. "If people mistake you for angels, do you have wings?"

"Yes and no."

I wait for him to continue, but he just smiles.

"Come on, tell me!"

He winks at me and jumps up. "Look, the tow truck is here!"

Bastard.

By the time we arrive in Oban, it's early afternoon. The mechanic had a look at the car's engine (he was a little surprised by the water damage) and told us he could have it fixed by tomorrow morning. That got me some very annoyed glances by the guys. We could have rented another car, but they were all too small to fit four large guys. And for protection reasons – they wouldn't expand on that – they refused to split up into two cars. So, we're stuck here for the night.

Oban is a lovely little seaside town, equipped for the thousands of tourists who come here every summer, both to stay and to take a ferry to one of the many islands on the Scottish West coast. Now, at the end of October, it's quiet and peaceful. The people passing us are mainly locals, and many of the tourist shops are already closed. I always enjoy seeing how a town transforms between seasons. It's like the façade the tourists see is slowly fading away until the real town emerges, before being hidden once again when spring arrives. Right now, we're at the point where both versions merge.

The last time I stayed in Oban was several years ago on a family holiday, so I walk around open-eyed, taking in the changes and the memories. Behind me, the guys are following, a little less enthusiastic.

"That's great, just great. She destroyed the car. I liked that car," Storm grumbles as he follows us to the MacCulloch Hotel's entrance. I really want to tell him to drop the topic, but that may be dangerous.

The woman at the front desk looks a little perplexed when Frost requests a family suite for us – and so must I, because Arc leans down and whispers, "If you have another flare, all four of us need to be there to contain it." I nod, uncomfortable at the thought of another magic explosion. If I set fire to the hotel, I could endanger dozens of people. Arc must have read my mind because he adds, "Don't worry, we'll make sure nothing happens."

Frost turns around from the very flushed looking reception clerk, dangling the keys in his hand like some sort of treasure. "We got the best suite in the house," he declares, waiting for praise that never comes. His usual frown reappears and he mutters something about 'no appreciation for his flirting skills'. We follow him into the old-fashioned elevator – everything is gold in there, although it's flaking at the edges. With me squashed into the middle and the four men all around me, we just about manage to fit into the lift. My body touches theirs in several places, and I can feel the heat rising in my face. Don't think of how close they are, Wyn. Think of something else... like butterflies. Something neutral, not sexy. Not hot. Not – aargh. I'm going to kill my hormones one of these days.

I'm relieved when the doors open with a ding, and I can escape the hotness. I'm talking about the temperature, honest.

Our suite is large, if a little run down. One king-sized bed, two smaller single beds and a sofa.

"I take the bed," Frost shouts and throws himself onto the bed. From the sound it makes, I'm sure he's just broken several springs in it.

"The princess gets the bed," Storm growls. What a gentleman. But this whole princess thing irritates me immensely.

"Would you stop calling me princess? I've never even been to the Realms and I know next to nothing about Beira and what she rules over. How can I be a princess if all I know is the human world? My magic is out of control, I have no clue what I'm doing, and..." My voice breaks a little. Damn it, I hadn't planned to show them how insecure I feel. My eyes are tearing up as I think of how silly I am, standing here in the middle of these Guardians who have no doubt got better things to do than looking after a self-pitying girl. I haven't cried this much in years, not since puberty and Tom Martin breaking up with me.

Arc is by my side in a flash and takes me into his arms. His thick muscles press against my ribcage and I lean into him, burying my face in his chest. He feels so warm and comfy; I don't want to let go. For a moment, I feel safe.

"Everything will get clearer when we get there, lassie," he whispers, his breath warm on my head. "Your mother will explain things, and you'll learn how to control your powers. You'll be magnificent once you know how to deal with them." He gently rubs my back and I almost let my tears flow. But I don't want to be even weaker in front of them. I detangle myself from his hug – regretting every inch I move away from his warmth – and step back until I reach the bed.

They're all looking at me, as if they're not quite sure how to deal with all the drama. Don't worry, boys, neither do I.

"You can take the bed, Frost, I'm the smallest. I'll take the sofa." It doesn't actually look that bad; it's long enough for me to lie comfortably without my legs hanging in the air. And it'll be a lot comfier for me than for the boys. Guess being small has its advantages.

"No, Storm is right," Frost says with a sigh. "You take the big bed."

Chapter Four

I wake up and I know I need to get outside. It's dark and judging from the light snoring coming from two different directions, everyone is still sleeping, but something important is happening and I need to leave this room, immediately. As quiet as I can, I slip out from under the covers and make my way through the dark room. A sliver of golden streetlamp light breaking through a slit in the curtains is the only thing illuminating the room, but somehow I know exactly where to tread without stumbling over our clothes or bags. Just when I reach the door, Arc lifts his head from the sofa closest to the exit. "What ye doin'?" he asks groggily.

Without being called for, my magic springs into life. "Sleep," I whisper, threads of magic carrying my command. He sinks back onto the sofa. I quickly step out of the room and follow the corridor to the elevator. I know I have to take it to -1, the underground garage. The lift is taking forever to arrive and hot sweat breaks out on my skin. I need to hurry up. For a moment, I debate taking the stairs, but then I remember that it's important to take the elevator. I don't want anyone to see me. Finally, the golden doors open and I step into the cabin. There are two men in there, dressed in black, but I ignore them. They're safe, no threat to me.

With a loud ding, the doors close, something hits me from behind and I black out.

"... We should kill her now, while she's unconscious."

"Boss wants to talk to her first."

"We have no idea what she's capable of. It might be safer to not take the risk."

My stomach lurches and my head is one big pain. Where the hell am I? The ground below me is vibrating. I'm in a car, the boot, apparently, but without a cover so I can see the daylight shining through the back window. I must have been out for hours. Trying not to make a sound, I shift my limbs, assessing the situation. No gag, no blindfold – either the movies are wrong or these kidnappers don't know how to do it right.

Best of all: They used rope to tie my hands together. How lovely. Handcuffs would have been a lot harder. I concentrate and send a single tendril of magic to the rope, willing it to burn quickly but without smoke. A bright blue flame erupts, dissolving the rope in seconds. My hands are free.

"Didn't you see how easy it was to control her mind? Sweet like a lamb being led to slaughter. If only every job was this simple."

"You didn't feel her magic. It's strong, even though she's untrained. She could rip us apart with a thought, Duke. We should kill her. I don't know how long the spell will keep her subdued."

Anger curses through me. How dare they. Breaking into my mind, manipulating me to walk straight to them like an imbecile. How could I not have known? I was supposed to be powerful, but then how could they overpower me so easily? It's time for revenge.

I sit myself up, smiling sweetly at them. "It no longer does," I chirp, before unleashing my magic. The guy on the wheel turns around, but I wrap him in icy strands of magic, rendering him immobile. At the same time, I shoot a blast of air towards the second guy, crashing his head on the dashboard. With a bang, the airbag inflates, pushing him back against the headrest. He's still, no longer moving. Good.

The car swerves. Not so good. With both men immobilised, the car is driving itself. Oops, I didn't think of that. We're racing along the road; luckily there are no other cars around. I can see a tree-lined junction in the distance where the road forked into two. I need to stop the car or we'll crash. I send out a tendril of wind magic towards the pedals. The man's foot is still on the accelerator. Concentrating hard, I push his foot away with a burst of wind and use my magic to press down on the breaks. It's not easy to keep the wind concentrated on such a small area without pressing down the other pedals. I can feel sweat pooling into tiny beads on my forehead. The car slithers and groans, but it slows down.

Too late. A tree crashes into the car - or do we crash into the tree? I am thrown forwards, suspended in the air as my magic bursts out of me, uncalled. I'm floating over the back row of the car, staring at the large branch that has broken through the windscreen, ready to impale me. I give my magic a mental hug. Without it, I'd be an unsightly human kebab by now. I ask it

55

to put me down and I gently float down to the scratchy car boot floor.

I crawl back into the boot, avoiding the evil branch that is blocking my way out. The back doors are bent; I doubt I can break them open.

I try to open the car boot door, but it's stuck, no matter how much I rattle at the door handle. I shoot a burst of wind against it, but all it does is throw me backwards. Damn it. Imprisoned in my kidnappers' car. Now there's a sad story for you. I'll need to think of something better than brute violence. Fire maybe? But then, using fire in a crashed car might not be the smartest idea ever. Who knows if there's leaked oil somewhere.

Would freezing metal do anything? Why not. I send some tendrils of frost magic to the edges of the boot door, thinking this might shrink the metal enough for it to open. Thin ice begins to cover the metal; little ice flowers that are making me smile. And when I kick the door and it actually opens, I smile even more. Fresh air, finally. I slowly untangle myself and climb out of the car.

Now that I'm outside, I can see the whole extent of the accident. A tree has dented the entire front of the car, and one massive branch has pierced through the windscreen. I check on the two men, but they are either out cold or dead. I decide not to check. As much as I want to do the right thing and get them help, they did try to kill me. One of them was really quite adamant about that.

I wish I had my phone with me to call the guys. Where are my Guardians when I need them?

In the distance, I can see a car approach. They'll surely stop and call the police when they see the accident. I decide to disappear; they might ask questions that I don't have an answer to. On my left, bushes cover a low ditch. Perfect. I crouch behind the undergrowth, watching as the car comes to a stop in front of me. An older man gets out, looks around, then takes out his phone. I assume he's dialling 999. While he listens to the operator's instructions and checks on the two men, I'm crawling along the ditch, further away from the scene of the accident.

How am I going to get away from here? We're in the middle of nowhere; all that surrounds us are green pastures with woolly white sheep. They're cute, but not much help in this situation. What I need is a phone. But then, I don't even have the guys' numbers.

When I'm a few hundred yards away from the crash, I stop, giving my aching body a chance to rest. I curse the flat landscape, making it impossible for me to get up and walk. The good samaritan would likely see me, and so would any police cars or ambulances coming this way. My only option is to wait until they've come, dealt with the accident and left. I try to find the least muddy bit of earth around me, and make myself comfortable. This is going to be a long wait, and I'm still in my pyjamas and slippers. I make a mental wish list: a jacket, warm shoes and a book. Oh, and a large thermos flask of tea, please. A portable heater wouldn't be bad, either.

I grin at my own joke. Yes, I've come far enough to laugh at my own pitiable humour. Oh well.

Fifteen minutes later, the ambulance arrives. A few minutes later, two police cars join it.

I stay in my ditch, shivering and miserable. I look down the road and see another car approach. I'm just about to duck so I stay hidden, but then I notice the four passengers crammed into the small car. Four big, beautiful, male passengers. I jump up and wave at them like a madwoman.

My guys have arrived.

Chapter Five

When we couldn't find you, we persuaded," Storm smiles grimly when he says that, "the hotel clerk to show us the CCTV footage. Luckily your kidnappers were either stupid or careless. Their number plate was in full view when they left the parking garage."

"How did the number plate help you?" I ask, confused.

"We've got... connections," Storm adds. "All major roads have cameras that continuously track the number plates of all cars driving along it. It was easy to see their route, until they started to use smaller roads – but then a call came through about an accident involving this very car."

"Don't ever scare us like that again," Arc grumbles.

I take the bait. "Or what?"

"Or I'll leash you and keep you within reach at all times." His voice turns dark as he says that, and I swallow hard. The other guys turn away from me, hiding their smiles. Evil.

"Do you still have your phone?" Frost asks as he takes out the sim card of his own and throws it out of the open window.

"No, course not, otherwise I would have been able to call you."

He nods sagely. "Guys, give me yours. We don't know who these guys were and what kind of resources they have."

"But I just bought mine," Crispin moans theatrically.

"Royal coffers, remember?"

"Ok, but be gentle with it." He pretends to cry as Frost breaks his phone in two. So much for gentle.

"Do you have anything else they could track?"

Nobody looks at Frost for a moment, then Arc sighs and takes off his watch. It's one of those fancy smart watches that can do all sorts of cool stuff. Yeah, not jealous at all.

"Sorry, mate," Frost grins, then conjures a sphere of water around the watch. Its display blinks a few times, then stays black. Death by drowning. Lovely. Arc looks wistfully at his broken watch. "Can I at least keep it?"

"Better safe than sorry," Frost says and throws it out of the window where it joins a pile of broken phones and sim cards. "Now all we need to do is get rid of the car."

"Thank the Gods," Storm calls from the driver's seat. "This thing is far too small. I'm not even sure if I can make it out of this seat without dislocating something."

"Where are we going to get a new car from?" I ask. "And where did you leave our old one?"

"When we saw that you were gone, we had to improvise." Frost avoids my eyes.

"So you stole it?"

"We borrowed it. We'll leave some cash in it for the owner."

"Well, that's very generous of you," I huff.

"Would you rather we had waited for the garage to repair our rental car? You'd still be sitting in the ditch had we not driven here straight away," Storm says angrily.

I decide to keep my mouth shut. In a way, he's right. But only in a way. I won't tell him that, I don't need to inflate his ego even more.

"We'll drive to the nearest village and get a new car. And then we'll drive to Ullapool without any delays. We need to get you to the Stones as soon as possible, especially with these people wanting you for some reason."

"At least *they* want me," I throw at him.

He's silent for a moment, then mumbles, "What gave you the idea I didn't want you?"

"You've not exactly been very friendly to me since we met."

Frost snickers, earning him a death glare from both Storm and myself. "Wyn, this is my brother at his friendliest. He's a lot less grumpy now that you're with us than usual."

I stare at him. "Are you serious? He's arrogant, impolite, ..."

"I can hear you!" Storm thunders.

"I know, that's why I'm saying it."

Arc interrupts. "As entertaining as this is, we need ta get going. I dinnae ken when the last ferry goes, so we'd better hurry."

That shuts us all up. The voice of reason, coming out of Arc's mouth. That's... refreshing.

Only twenty minutes later, we sit in a new car, a dark green Toyota. It's bigger than the last one, but I'm still squeezed by the two brutes sitting on either side of me. Storm is driving, as always, and his brother is sitting next to him, studying a map he found in the glove compartment. Which leaves me with Crispin and Arc on the back bench. Arc is slightly hunched, preventing his head from bumping against the ceiling. I'm pressed against Crispin, trying to give Arc more space. I don't think we're going to be able to stay in this position for very long.

"Luckily those bastards took you in the right direction," Frost says, pointing at the map. "We would have lost a lot of time otherwise. But now we're only about an hour away from Ullapool where we'll take the ferry to Stornoway. From there it's about half an hour's drive to the Stones, so we should be at the Gate before night falls."

"What will happen once we get there?" I ask.

"We'll open the Gate and step through to the Realms."

"You make it sound very easy."

"It is. Piece of cake. Unless there are demons. Or Gods. Or, even worse, girls."

I turn to Crispin. "Did he just say 'girls'?"

He grins and loud-whispers, "The twins got a bit of a fan club. Some of the female Guardians and humans living in the border area of the Realm—"

"Wait, there are humans living in the Gods' Realms?"

"Aye," Arc says, grimacing. "Some Gods like to have... pets."

"They keep humans as pets?" I cringe. Maybe I don't want to visit my mother after all.

"Not those kinds of pets. Think more of... well..."

"Sex, lassie," Arc barges in, grinning happily. "Apparently, humans are quite good in bed."

I blush, wiping from my mind the image of naked humans surrounding a Goddess on her throne. "Does that mean Gods aren't?"

I resist asking about Guardians. I don't want to give them the impression of a needy human female who hasn't been with a man in far too long.

"There aren't many Gods around," Crispin explains, "and some prefer not to mix work with pleasure, so Guardians are out of the running. Humans are a logical choice."

"How many Gods are there?"

"How can ye not ken?" Arc shoots me an incredulous look.

"Hey, I was brought up human. It's not my fault my mother didn't teach me anything about her world."

That shuts them up.

"Lass, she had her reasons," Arc finally says softly. I nod, looking out of the window, avoiding his glance. It's a sore point and I'd rather avoid crying in front of them. I don't cry very often, but somehow I feel like my hormones are in turmoil. Must be all this testosterone around me.

We drive on in silence, slowly getting closer to a new chapter in my life.

Chapter Six

It's late afternoon by the time we arrive in Ullapool. We have no time to explore its pretty little streets as we drive straight into the maw of the ferry (seriously, it looks like a massive sea monster with its mouth wide open ready to swallow the cars and lorries that are waiting to board). The ferry is much bigger than I thought. There are several food outlets, a shop and even a tiny cinema. We head to a quiet corner in a pub-style restaurant. I have a quick look at the menu, but the movement of the ship is making me feel queasy already - I don't even want to think about how it'll feel once we leave the harbour. Instead of food, I order a whisky. The guys look at me strangely when I order a glass of the 12-year-old Highland Park, but I ignore them. Not every person under 25 drinks their whisky mixed with coke or other travesties. I add a single drop of water, gleefully watching the Guardians' faces. This is fun. Whisky has never tasted this good.

They have all ordered food, and by the time it arrives, the boat has left Ullapool and the waves have started to become bigger. The floor is vibrating from the movement of the engines, and together with the smell of the food it's beginning to make me feel nauseous.

I excuse myself and head to the toilets. I don't have to puke (not yet, anyway), but I need to get away from the food. Okay, maybe the toilets weren't the best idea. Judging from the smell permeating the small room, nobody has cleaned them in a while. Or a lot of other people have been sick already, which I kind of doubt. I stumble back through the heaving corridors until I reach a lounge. Comfortable airline-style seats are inviting me to rest, but instead I step through a heavy door out onto the deck. I breathe in the fresh air - it's only slightly smelling of exhaust fumes - and go to the railings, looking down into the dark, foamy water. A few other people are standing outside, mostly smokers having a fag.

With every breath, my nausea dissipates. Guess I'll spend the rest of the journey outside. I stick my hands into the large front pocket of my hoodie. I need to thank the guys later on for bringing my clothes from the hotel. Taking off my mud-crusted pyjamas was the best thing I did all day.

Gulls are circling the ship, white dots in a cloud-hung sky. I wonder if they'll accompany us all the way to the islands. I close my eyes, breathing in the salty sea air. Below me, the engines hum a steady song. The enormity of this journey finally begins to sink in. I'm going to visit my mother. I'm actually going to see the Realms of the Gods. I've dreamed of travelling there all my life, and now it's finally time. I'm going back to the place I was born, and get to know the woman who gave birth to me. Maybe she'll even tell me about my father. On all her visits, and in her letters, she's refused to tell me who he is. All I know is that he isn't a God - but that doesn't really help, does it.

With the engine noise filling my ears, I don't notice the quiet around me until it's too late. I open my eyes and realise that I'm the only one left on the deck. It's eerily quiet, and the gulls have disappeared. I turn to walk back inside, but I don't even make it a single step. I am thrown into the air by an invisible fist squeezing my waist. I tumble and fall, screaming, and then the sea comes closer, too close, black and blue and foreboding, and the wind drops me into the water, pushing me under. I fight, freeing my magic, pushing against the foreign, black tendrils that are wrapped around my body. My eyes are filled with seawater, but somehow I know that this strange, hostile magic is all around me. Instinctively, I weave a net of my magic all over my skin, then push, ignoring my burning lungs, until the net becomes a sphere around me, keeping the stranger's magic away from me. It takes all my strength to keep the shield up and use my arms and legs to try and reach the surface of the water that is threatening to drown me. Black spots are clouding my vision and my lungs are going to force open my mouth any second now. I'm going to drown. Finally, I reach the surface, taking in a big breath, almost swallowing half a wave in the process. I cough, trying to stay afloat while struggling for air. My energy is rapidly leaving me. I'll have to decide between keeping the magic net up or swimming. I choose swimming.

When the magic tendrils pull back into my body, a shiver runs through me, bringing a tiny bit of extra energy with it. Enough to stay afloat for a little while longer. I shake my head, trying to get the salt water out of my eyes so I can see. Waves are towering over me on all sides, but in between them I can see the ferry, disappearing slowly. Nobody seems to have noticed that I went overboard. What now? I can just about see land in the direction we came from, but I'd never reach it. Even if I knew how to use my magic to swim faster, I wouldn't have the energy. I'm getting tired of being faced with certain death. It's happened far too often in the past few days. In this moment, I wish the Gods were like the beings many humans expect them to be: all-knowing, all-seeing, able to rescue people from danger. Instead, they're probably drunk in some palace in an alternate reality. They couldn't care less about humans. And even if they did, it's not like they could see me from their Realm.

Fuck it. I'm going to live. In a sudden burst of inspiration, I form a small fireball floating above me, away from the reach of the waves, then throw it into the sky, like a flare. It's not very bright, but I'm sure it can be seen from the ferry. Just in case, I pull together every last bit of magic I have in me and make a second ball of fire, slightly bigger. I let it float upwards, trying to make it last as long as possible. I almost cry when my last hope fizzles out above me. But then, what's the point in crying when your cheeks are already wet with salt water from the sea that is going to drown you.

With every wave carrying me up and letting me drop, my hope wanes. I think of my parents, the humans who raised me. They'll be waiting for me to return, thinking I'm happily spending time with my birth mother, when in fact I'm lying at the bottom of the sea.

A shout rips through the roaring of the waves. I try to keep my head out of the water to listen. Again, a shout, this time closer.

I open my mouth to reply, but a wave breaks over my head and I am shoved down into the depths. When I resurface again, I manage to shout, although it comes out more like a hoarse whisper, "Here! I'm here!"

"WYN! Wynter!" Frost. He's come for me.

"Hee—" Another wave swallows my shout, but a second later he is there, hovering on the waves like a surfer. In any other situation I'd admire the effortless way he seems to stand on the water, the beauty of his toned body against the light of the waning sun, the shadows on his face highlighting his masculine features... But in this moment, I'm drowning and I don't care. Sue me.

He kneels by my side - yes, he effing kneels on the water that is trying to devour me - and pulls me up until I'm in his arms, pressed against his heaving chest.

"Are you hurt?" His voice is tense and I want to tell him that I'm alright, that I will be alright, but all that comes out is a pitiful cough. He hugs me even tighter and begins to run over the water's surface, back towards the ferry. His body is warm and I snuggle against him, listening to his heart beat as I close my eyes.

Somehow, we get back to the ferry. It involves him running on the water's surface, slaloming around waves and clouds of spray. I stay snuggled against Frost's broad chest, shivering and only half-conscious. Too. Much. Water. For. One. Day.

And far too much magic. At least this time it wasn't my own magic that tried to kill me. Which leads to the question what this assassination attempt was all about, but I can't think. My head hurts.

W hen we arrive at the ferry, I can see the other three guys standing on deck by the railing, looking down on us. Storm holds up his hands and a wind hose forms around us, gently picking us up (together with a lot of ocean) and carrying us all the way to the deck they're standing on. Strong arms take me away from Frost. I resist, I want to stay with him.

"Shhh, it's ok, he just needs a moment of rest." I let go of Frost, and the warmth. But I'm handed to another warm body I can snuggle against. Another warm chest presses against my back until I'm sandwiched between two of my Guardians. Now, I understand why they're called that. They worked together and actually rescued me. I feel a little pathetic; the damsel in distress. I'm supposed to be the strong one, the one who's more powerful than them. Right now, I don't feel powerful at all. But inside, a little voice reminds me how much I enjoy being hugged by the guys.

Now that I'm out of the water and standing in the cold evening air, I feel the cold seeping into my bones. If the guys weren't holding me up, I'd probably collapse to the ground from exhaustion. My magic is depleted; only now I notice how much of a part it is inside me. It's like there's a hole inside my chest, just to the right of my heart. I hope it refills quickly.

"Let's get you out of the cold," Crispin says gently from behind me. He lifts me up and carries me in his arms, back inside. Arc is walking ahead of us, leading us until we reach a large door. It's dark inside but he switches on the light as we enter - and we're standing in a small cinema. It's actually more like a big tv screen with a few rows of chairs in front of it.

"The projector is broken, so we'll be undisturbed in here for now," he explains. Crispin carries me to the front row and gently puts me down on one of the chairs. I must look desperate to get back into his warm arms, because he says, "we need to get you out of your clothes first, Princess. You'll not get warm otherwise."

Even in my diminished state of mind, alarm bells are starting to ring. Getting naked. In front of the guys. No way. It's bad enough Crispin has seen me in my underwear already.

Storm gives me a stern glance and takes charge. "Arc, go to the car and get her some clothes from her bag. Frost, you're soaked as well. Strip, Arc can get you something new to wear. Crispin, check her for injuries once she's undressed."

"What? No, definitely not," I protest. "You're all going to leave the room and then I'll change. No nudeness, no examining, no staring. Get it?"

Arc starts to laugh, but I frown at him until he turns and leaves the room. Got rid of one, three more to go.

"I'm happy to strip together with you if that makes it easier," Frost snickers, lifting an eyebrow suggestively. No thanks.

I ignore the rush of heat in my cheeks and other body parts. This is awkward.

The shivering is getting worse and my teeth are beginning to chatter noticeably. When I cough, Storm is by my side in a moment, pulling me out of my seat.

"Clothes off, now," he growls through clenched teeth.

Shocked, I stare at him. He sighs. "Frost, take her."

"I'm busy stripping as you commanded, brother dear," Frost chuckles, standing there with all his clothes still on, watching us with amusement. He's making no moves to actually take off his wet shirt or - Gods forbid - trousers.

"Crisp, you do it." Storm shoves me in the blond guy's direction.

"I'll need my hands for the healing," Crispin replies, smiling innocently.

Storm's expression is changing from stern to desperate.

"Fine, I'll do it. Lift up your arms, Princess."

"Stop calling me princess, I'm Wyn. And no, I won't." I cross my arms in front of my chest. One exasperated sigh later, my arms are in the air, held up there in Storm's iron grip. I shriek and try to get away from him, but he's not letting me go. I weakly kick his shin, but all that gets me is his legs capturing my own between his, squeezing them so I can't move and am no longer standing, but hanging from my arms. What. The. Fuck. This guy is crazy.

The other two are bent over laughing. Once I've killed Storm, they'll be next. My wrath will be terrible. When my magic returns.

Storm changes his grip until he holds my arms in one hand, then uses the other hand to lift up my top. I squeal as my belly is exposed to the guys. I struggle, but all the movement is making me light-headed. Maybe I should have let Crispin check me out first.

"Stop struggling," Storm growls, squeezing my legs harder with his own. Harder. Hard. No, don't think of that. This is not a sexual thing. This is survival of the fittest.

Storm is fighting with my shirt - luckily, my boobs are forming a natural hill that the wet fabric is refusing to slide over. Thanks boobs. Glad you're on my side. And the fact that my nipples are hard is not a sign of treachery, but of the cold. Definitely.

"Let me help," Frost murmurs from behind me and slides his warm hands under my shirt. I can feel him touching my bra strap, wandering higher, squeezing my shoulders. He leans against me and instinctively, I stop fighting his brother and lean back until my back touches his chest.

"You're not supposed to grope her, you're supposed to help me strip her," Storm complains.

"Isn't that the same thing?"

"Fuck it." Storm lets me fall against his brother - who catches me, luckily - and puts his hands on my neckline, ripping my shirt apart until I'm standing there in my bra and something that looks like a bolero.

"What the hell do you think you're doing?" I scream as I try to cover myself with my arms. At least that's what I want to do, but Frost takes them and presses them against my sides.

"You don't have anything to hide," he whispers, his breath hot against my ear. The resistance inside me melts a tiny bit. Why does his voice have to be so... sexy.

Before I can do anything, he gently pushes me forward until I'm pressed against his brother's chest. Frost slides the ruined shirt down my back until there's nothing left on my skin but the bra. His hands slide over my skin, warm and gentle. Goosebumps break out on my arms. This feels good and wrong at the same time. I'm standing in my bra in front of three men I've only just met.

"Oh, I see you've started without me!" Arc's deep voice echoes through the cinema.

Ok, make that four men. Maybe this would be a good moment to feel like a slut. Or to scream. Or to just give in... no. Not happening.

Arc is walking down the steps towards us, his eyes hungrily taking in my body. This big, sweet guy has just turned into a hot, sexy predator.

I stop squirming and just look at him, trapping his gaze with my own. Frost takes that moment to unclasp my bra. I'm still pressed against Storm's chest, which is holding it in place. But I can see from the evil grin on Arc's face that this is not going to be the case for much longer. He joins the twins, which means I'm now sandwiched between three guys. Crispin is holding back, just watching us. That doesn't mean that he looks unaffected though.

I shiver involuntarily.

Arc steps even closer and cups my cheek with one hand. "You're freezing, Wyn. You should really get out of those clothes."

"We've been trying to tell her that, but she won't listen," Frost complains, humour sparkling in his voice.

"I am not. Getting. Naked. In front of you," I repeat, but it comes out in a bit of a moan as Frost's hands suddenly cup my breasts from behind. He gently squeezes them, rubbing my nipples through the thin fabric of my bra. Thank the Gods for that. Not for the squeezing, I mean. Just for the fabric. Really.

Arc kneels down on my side, pushing Storm away until he's in front of me. His hands go to the top of my trousers and I really should protest, but I really don't want to. He slowly unzips my jeans and I take in a heavy breath. Frost is still kneading my boobs and I lean back against him - and my bra slips down, leaving his hands on my naked skin. Ooops. Storm is staring at my chest, his face an unreadable mask. I look up at him, unsure. Then a smile begins to lift his cheeks, before his mouth crashes down on mine, pushing me further back into Frost's embrace. His lips are hard and soft at the same time and they claim me with a force that makes my heart flutter even more than it has already. I moan against him and open my mouth, making way for his tongue. In another part of my mind, I know that Arc is pulling down my trousers, and that Frost's erection is pressing hard against my back while he's playing with my nipples, but all I can focus on is the taste of Storm, his lips on mine, his tongue exploring my mouth.

When he breaks away, I'm breathless (and speechless). My knees feel weak, but I tell myself that it's due to my exhaustion, not the most amazing kiss I've ever been given.

Slowly, my awareness of the rest of my body returns. Something is pulsing deep between my legs as I feel all three guys touching my body in different places. There's something missing though. Someone. I move until I can see Crispin, standing on his own a few metres away from us. Our eyes meet and he gives me a sad smile.

I don't know what my mouth is thinking, but I whisper, "Come here."

He stays still for a moment and I'm close to accepting that he won't join us, but then his smile turns determined and he moves towards us.

And then the worst possible thing happens.

The tannoy cracks loudly. "We will shortly arrive in Stornoway harbour. May passengers please return to their cars."

A collective sigh goes through the room. I may have been part of it. Just when my body had finally overruled my mind.

Arc clears his throat and gets up from the floor. "We better get a move on."

"Yeah," Frost says, giving my breasts one last gentle squeeze before stepping away from me.

I am left with just Storm, who looks down at me sternly. "You should have changed." Then he steps away from me, leaving me bewildered.

Arc hands me my fresh clothes; a simple black t-shirt and white linen trousers. Without speaking, the guys turn around, making me stare at them in surprise. Now they let me change undisturbed? I can't believe it.

I quickly put on the shirt (Arc forgot to bring me a dry bra), take off my wet shoes and step out of the jeans that are pooled around my feet. I look at the dry clothes next to me. Oh no.

"No panties?"

"Ehm, didn't think you'd need them." Arc laughs and I'm sure it was deliberate. Bastard.

I groan in frustration.

"You should have brought her panties, mate," Frost says, surprising me.

"Why, are ye having a problem with the thought of her being naked underneath her trousers?" Arc teases.

"You're wearing a kilt. Do you know how uncomfortable this is?" Frost points at the bulge between his legs.

I'm going to try and forget that I heard this conversation.

Chapter Seven

It's dark by the time we roll off the ferry and head into Stornoway. Even though it's called the capital of the Western Isles, it's not very big, maybe a few thousand residents. We drive along the streets until we find a hotel that looks bright and inviting. The guys have decided that we need some rest, so we're staying the night rather than driving straight on to Calanais.

Storm heads inside to find out if they have a room available while the rest of us stay in the car.

"Is Storm your leader?" I ask, remembering how it's always the brooding, black-clad twin who organises everything.

"Aye, he's the boss," Arc grins. "When we let him."

"So it's not an official thing?"

"Nah, he's the oldest so he thinks he's in charge. And most of the time that's ok with the rest of us."

"He's older by a few minutes," Frost grumbles. "Just because our God couldn't create two Guardians at the same time."

"Why did he make you twins?" I ask. I still can't get my head around this whole concept of being created, not born.

"Guess it looks nicer if you're standing in between two strong, handsome Guardians that look the same," he snickers. "He was still practicing with Storm. By the time he made me, he'd reached perfection."

I snicker. "You sure about that?"

"Oi"! He punches me playfully. "I am the prettiest Guardian in the Realms."

"Ignore him," Crispin chimes in. "I won that title three times in a row."

"Because your God organised it!"

Storm's return interrupts their squabble (and stops me from trying to decide who of the four guys is the hottest one). He leads us inside and up some dark, velvet-lined stairs. "They didn't have a family room so we've got two doubles."

I sigh. "They didn't have twin rooms?"

"After what happened on the ferry, I didn't think you'd want a twin room," Storm says, his voice dark with a husky undertone.

"What happened on the ferry?! That was you molesting me!"

"We undressed you," he says flatly. "And you kissed me."

"What the fuck? It was you who kissed me!"

"And you kissed me back."

I'm speechless. And beaten. Yes, I kissed him back. Yes, I enjoyed it. Yes, I would probably do it all again. And more. I get flushed just thinking of it. A tiny voice inside me tells me that this isn't me, that this isn't natural, but I push it aside.

I can't give in though. "No, I didn't."

"Oh yes you did." Before I can even move, Storm grips my arms and presses me against the wall of the corridor, slamming his mouth onto mine, kissing me hard. My lips open to invite him in. Traitors.

"Ehm, could we do this inside our rooms? I don't want to attract attention," Frost's voice comes from far away. I don't care; I'm too busy kissing. I evade Storm's nudging tongue and slowly run my own along his teeth. So perfect.

He leans back, ending the kiss. My mouth follows him, taking the rest of my body with it. He steps back, his eyes filled with heat and regret. "Not here, Princess. Not like this." His voice is almost soft.

He turns and walks away, the other guys following him, leaving me standing there, bewildered. What the hell just happened? Did I let him kiss me? Again?

"Come on, Wyn," Crispin shouts from the other end of the corridor. I shake off my confusion (at least I try to) and hurry after them.

W e've got two rooms opposite from each other. They're identical; small, a little dark, but generally friendly looking. I enter the room to my right, where the guys are waiting for me. Arc is sprawled out on the king-size bed and if I bent down a little, I could probably look up his kilt... but no, that would be naughty.

Storm and Frost are standing by the window, talking quietly, while Crispin looks a little forlorn on his own in the middle of the room. He's the only one acknowledging me entering the room, though.

"How are you feeling?" he asks, putting an arm around my shoulders. The familiarity surprises and excites me at the same time. Crispin is still a bit of an enigma to me. He's the quietest one, always gentle, always standing slightly apart from the others. Frost and Storm match because of their looks (and their demeanour, I'm slowly starting to see, even though at first I thought them to be very different from each other), and Arc is similar enough to join their team. But Crispin... he's different. Not in a bad way, though. I just feel like there's a lot more to him than I can see on the surface.

"Tired," I reply, not wanting to tell him that I'm feeling absolutely shattered. I don't want him to think that he needs to heal me.

"Guys, let's talk. Wyn is exhausted, so let's get this over with as soon as possible."

"She's not the only one," Frost mumbles. Dark shadows are surrounding his eyes and his shoulders are slumped. Rescuing me from the grip of the sea must have taken more energy from him than I had realised. How did I not notice this before? Oh yes, he was touching my boobs. That's why.

"Arc, make some space," Storm commands, and the kilted Scot sits up on the bed. We join him on the springy mattress. That reminds me, we haven't discussed sleeping arrangements yet. I wish these men were smaller, so they could all fit on one bed. In the other room. Leaving this room for me.

"Ouch, you're sitting on my leg," Frost complains and pushes his brother. Which ends up in everyone shuffling around, making the springs underneath the mattress groan in anger. Maybe that's just my interpretation - and my projection, because a second later, Arc grabs me and puts me on his lap.

"See, now we have more space," he grins. I'm too tired to even protest. Besides, he's warm and comfy. His abs are hard beneath me, and I try to ignore that as best as I can.

Storm tssks, then clears his throat importantly. "Okay, let's begin. Wyn, did you see who threw you off the ferry?"

I shake my head. "No, the deck was empty. It was magic, it felt like the air grabbed me and pushed me over."

"Air magic... that complicates things."

"Why?"

"Not many mages have that ability," Storm explains. "It's more common in Guardians."

"Oh. But we can't exclude it being a mage, right?"

"No, but it's unlikely. Has anyone ever tried to harm you before? When you were still living among humans?"

"No, and why would they? Why is someone trying to kill me now?"

"They must have been waiting until your magic developed when you came of age," Storm says, ignoring my questions.

"We can't go on like this," Frost says tiredly. "She's almost been killed twice in one day, not counting the flares. From now on, two of us should always be with her."

"Two of you? Don't I get a say in this?"

"No," Storm says in his favourite grumble voice.

"I don't think that's enough," Crispin sighs. "If they break into her mind again, we may not be able to stop her from leaving. We need a failsafe."

"Are you thinking...?"

Arc shakes his head. "I don't think that's a good idea. The effects are already quite strong, and that would only make it... more intense."

"I agree," Storm grumbles.

"You would, wouldn't you. But it's not about you, it's about Wyn," Frost snaps. "Just because you can't control yourself, you'd put her in danger?"

I've had enough. "What the hell are you talking about?"

A collective silence answers me. "Ok, if you don't want to tell me, I'm going to bed. I'm taking the other room, you can stay here."

I sit up and untangle my legs from Crispin (who put his own over them at some point). Before I can leave, Arc's arms hug my belly and pull me back against him. "Let me go!"

"No," he whispers, and turns me until I'm looking straight into his emerald eyes. His gaze captivates mine and my breath catches in my throat. There's a tingling in my belly that tells me to lean forward, to press my lips against his and...

"What are you doing to me?" I whisper, in shock about my own thoughts. This is so not me.

"That's what we're talking about. The *pull*."

"Is that what is making me want to..."

"Kiss me? Fuck me? Yes." Arc's voice is hoarse and his pupils are dilated. I can feel him growing hard against my thighs. His lips are waiting for me, red and soft and delicious. I wonder what they feel like.

"Snap out of it," Storm growls and pulls me off Arc. Immediately, the spell is broken. I look at Arc in shock. Was I really about to kiss him? Gods, this is so wrong. I kissed Storm earlier tonight, now almost Arc, and when I look at the other two Guardians, I can easily imagine pressing my lips against theirs.

Crispin's calm voice pulls me out of my thoughts. "When Guardians absorb a God's magic, they form a bond with them. That's why it's forbidden. But you're different, you're a demi-goddess, so we thought it might be different. We didn't have a choice, when your magic flared, it was the only thing that stopped you from killing yourself."

"So when you stopped the earthquake... you pulled magic from me?"

"Yes, we absorbed as much as we could. Your mother was wise to send all four of us; one or two Guardians wouldn't have been enough. As long as you don't have full control over your magic, we need to be there in case it overwhelms you."

"Does this mean that my mother knew about the... side effects?"

"Nobody knew exactly what would happen, if there would be a bond at all, if the pull would be strong. You're the first demi-goddess in a long time. But yes, Beira knew it was a possibility."

I'm in shock. My mother was aware that I might fall for - no, that *my body* might fall for the Guardians she sent, and she did it anyway. What was she thinking? How could she do this to me? She was basically taking away my free will.

"But what if I never actually wanted to... kiss you? What if the bond forces me to do other things... isn't that like rape?"

Crispin shakes his head violently, but a slight grin is spreading on his face. "Oh, did I forget to mention? It isn't always a sexual pull the bond forces. That only happens when there is already an attraction that the bond can latch onto."

I switch on the tap and splash some cold water on my face. It doesn't make my head any clearer though. My mind is buzzing, my body is still in the grip of my manipulated hormones, and - well, let's just say that I'm a mess. On the other side of the bathroom door, four Guardians are impatiently waiting for me. We still haven't discussed what Crispin proposed. Not that I actually know what it is, just that it might help me from getting killed. Which makes it a good thing.

I sigh and dry my hands, noticing that they are shaking slightly. I could do with one of my mum's herbal tea infusions that she always made me before exams. Mum... I wonder what she's doing now. Are my parents alright? Are they still in the hotel the guys left them at? I wish I could call them to find out, but I can already imagine Storm's reply – something about safety, and phones being tracked.

Crispin told me that they'd wake up after about a day from the deep sleep he put them in. Their human minds needed time to process it all. Had he asked me, I could have told him that their human minds have been processing magic for the past twenty-two years. Right now, I wish they were here, putting me to bed, telling me that everything was going to be alright.

Instead, I have four Guardians who may look pretty good, but who I don't know at all.

When I walk back in to the room, the guys are no longer on the bed. Crispin is rummaging through their bags, while the other three are pushing the furniture around to make more space in the middle of the room.

Arc looks up when he hears the bathroom door close behind me. "We'll need to do some preparations for the ritual—"

"What ritual?" I almost shout. I'm exhausted and I want them to finally tell me what this is all about. All this secretive stuff is driving me crazy.

"There's a way how we can make sure that ye are okay, no matter if we're with ye or not. It's a bit like a GPS locator, except that in emergencies we can also talk to ye. That way we can get to ye much faster than with any other method."

"So you're saying you'll be able to talk in my mind?"

"Only when ye let us. It's a one-way connection that only you can open. So, if something bad was to happen, ye can open yer mind and talk to us, but we won't be able to hear you if ye don't."

"That doesn't sound so bad... so what's the downside?"

He looks a bit uncomfortable. "We dinnae ken if the bond will get stronger. Ye might be even more affected."

"No way. Absolutely. No. Way."

"It's the only way, lass. I dinnae want ye to die."

That shuts me up. Arc doing puppy eyes is just evil. Here's this big, tough, kilt-wearing guy, looking at me like I'm... well, special to him?

"But... I'm reacting the same to all of you. How can I feel like this all the time, around four guys? What if I... kiss one of you, and later another? That's not fair on any of us."

"Nah, don't think like that. Storm and Frost have shared all their life. Not sure aboot Crisp, but I enjoyed watching ye with Storm. And having ye on my lap. And on the ferry. We should do that again."

I blush. No, we definitely should not. Or maybe we should. I don't know what to think anymore. How much of it is the bond and how much is me? Can I still trust my thoughts? What if it's even worse after the ritual? Will I become a lovesick demi-goddess lusting after her Guardians?

Even now, standing so close to Arc, I can feel the pull towards him. My body is wanting to touch him.

"It's getting worse. How is it getting worse if you haven't pulled any energy from me since the earthquake?"

Arc is silent for a moment, then murmurs, "We think it's because we're around each other all the time. Your magic is reacting to the magic residue in our bodies."

Eww, that sounds gross for some reason. But at least there's a simple solution.

"So if I stay away from you it gets better? Then I'll just take a bus to Calanais, walk through the stones and be done with it. No need for you all to be around me."

He looks at me with a pained expression. "I hadn't realised ye disliked us so much."

"I don't dislike you, on the contrary! But I feel like I'm being manipulated from all sides, and I hate feeling so powerless. I need to be able to make my own decisions, not let some strange bond make them for me." A sob escapes my throat. Don't cry. Please don't cry in front of the guys. I'm looking weak enough as it is, having to be rescued all the time.

Arc opens his arms and invites me in. I hug him back. Ok, let's be weak for a second. Arc's hugs are the best.

For once, the bond lets us enjoy this simple, non-sexual hug. Thank you, magic.

"We're ready," Frost announces. They've removed the rugs that were covering the floor, exposing the worn wooden boards underneath. Storm is putting the finishing touches to an intricate design drawn on the floor with a liquid that looks like black ink. Except that it's a bit like gel, less fluid than ink.

Storm wipes his black-stained hands on his jeans. Pray for whoever is going to do his laundry.

I take a closer look at the drawing. It's like a large Celtic knot, never-ending and endlessly wound, but there's another knot on top, and another, until they form a rough circle. Just like you can draw a star by putting two triangles on top of each other, he's made a circle from Celtic knots (my mum would disagree, of course, being an artist and all).

"Don't touch it," Storm warns as I step closer.

"What is it? Is it like a pentagram?"

"Pentagrams aren't magical, only charlatans use it." Frost comes over to inspect his brother's handiwork. I can feel his breath on my neck as he stands behind me. "This one here is the real deal. Well done, brother dear."

"Yes, it's pretty, but what does it actually do?" I ask impatiently. Hey, it's my mind they're going to mess with.

In response, Storm lifts me up and unceremoniously puts me down in the middle of the knot-circle-thingy.

"So now I'm allowed to touch it?" I ask incredulously. That barbarian, picking me up like his play toy. I've got free will. Most of the time. Unless my hormones start doing their thing.

"Don't move. If you distort the pattern all sorts could happen."

"But what is going to happen?" Gods, do I sound whiney. But I've got a point.

Crispin gives me a reassuring smile. "Nothing bad. We're going to focus our energies into the knot, and they will flow through it, mixing and binding together with your own. It won't hurt, don't worry. It might feel a little strange though, but as I said, it's nothing bad."

"Okay. What do I need to do?"

"You stand there and look pretty," Frost snickers, but shuts up when his brother shoots him an evil glance. Phew, I'm glad he's not looking at me like that - for now, at least.

"Close your eyes—"

"And think of me," I interrupt and the other guys burst out laughing. "Sorry, please continue."

Storm huffs. "Close your eyes and concentrate on your magic. Imagine where it sits in your body and focus your mind on that place. Got that?"

I relax, turning my thoughts inward until I can feel the spot to the right of my heart where my magic lives. Right now, it's lying in there, curled up like a cat, but slightly tense, looking wistfully at the guys' magic. The bond is affecting it.

"Now open your magic and invite ours in," Storm's soft voice comes from far away.

"How do I do that?" I whisper.

"Imagine earlier... our kiss... how you invited me in... how you opened your mouth for me... how I entered you with my tongue... how I suckled on your lips... how you were ready for me..."

My magic is purring at his words. Yes girl, I like hearing it too. Doesn't mean that I have to go all pouncy about it all. She's opening herself, getting up with a yawn and a stretch, then expands, leaving the cave close to my heart and entering my body. My veins rejoice as the magic flows through them. My head feels light and heavy at the same time. I see colours explode in front of my closed eyes, and an orchestra plays a serenade all around me. Okay, maybe that's a little exaggeration. But seriously, this feeling is ... magical.

"Yes, that's it, beautiful. Just a little more, you're almost there. Think of how much you want us. Relax into the feeling, Princess."

I moan mentally (luckily my mouth doesn't betray me this time) and let go of the last strings that are holding my magic back. She pounces and jumps out of me, into the waiting arms of... well, what are they? Four balls of rainbow light are glowing all around me. If a unicorn had broken wind, that's what it might look like. I still have my eyes closed, but somehow I can still see them, their magic, flowing out of them into the knot I'm standing on. From the ground, delicate rainbow tendrils are reaching up, gently moving towards me. My magic goes out to greet them and invites them in like long-lost friends. When their magic flows into me, fireworks explode in my mind. A cacophony of feelings threatens to overwhelm me: love, passion, laughter, hate, tears, empathy, sadness, mourning, admiration. For most of the feelings, I have no words. They are simply... there. Introducing themselves to me. With them come images, sounds, smells. Memories. I don't have time to take a proper look, but I file them away for later.

My magic is glowing with happiness as she slowly returns to my heart cave. She plumps onto the ground, licking her paws with delight. One satisfied little magic. Around her, colours are sparkling in the darkness. She's surrounded by something new.

I smile as I realise how this completes me. I never knew it was missing, but now that I can see the colours, I know that there was too much darkness in that cave before. Now it's all light and sunshine and unicorn farts.

With a final yawn, my magic lays her head on her paws and closes her eyes, a satisfied look on her pristine face. And with her happy, I am happy too.

Tiredness overwhelms me as I can see her fall asleep. And just like her, I lie down and curl up, wrapping my non-existing tail around me as I slip into a restful sleep.

Chapter Eight

P rincess, it's time to wake up."

No, it certainly isn't. It's the middle of the night, and if it isn't on your clock, then it certainly is in my mind. My inner clock shows three in the morning. Let me sleep.

"Wyn, we need to go."

Don't bother me. I'm busy. Sleeping is important.

My duvet is pulled away. I pull it back over my head. Suddenly something presses on my back and bum. Something big and heavy.

"She can't get up if you're sitting on her, Arc!"

"But maybe this will make her want to get up."

I groan. Boys. What have I done to deserve this? Oh yes, I burned down a house and organised a little earthquake. I forgot. Intentionally.

Arc shifts on top of me, making my hip bones grind against the hard mattress.

"Get off me," I complain, my voice hoarse with sleep. "You're hurting me."

The weight is gone immediately. I look up and see Frost and Storm holding a bewildered looking Arc, while Crispin is next to my bed. "Are you in pain?"

"What? No... I just said that to get him off me."

"Oh." He looks a bit unsure. "No side effects then?"

"Should there be any?"

He grimaces. "Well, one book said that there might be a headache after the ritual, but—"

I sit up with a start and hold a hand up in front of his face. "And you didn't feel like I should know?" I snarl, giving them all my most evil look.

Crispin coughs uncomfortably. "It was only one book, and you're fine, so no need to worry."

"See, I told ya you shouldn't tell her," Arc grimaces in sympathy.

"From now on you're going to tell me everything. Side effects, problems, suspected troubles, everything. Capisce?"

Four guys are looking at me, then nod one by one. I'm a bit bewildered at how easily they gave in. That's unusual. Then I notice the fireballs around my hands. Oh. So they're scared of me. How cute. I wave my hands through the air, fascinated by how the fire stays in place without burning me. Hell, I wouldn't even have noticed it was there.

"Could you switch that off, please?" Frost asks with a worried frown. He probably remembers what happened last time I used fire magic. My feeling of awe dissipates. He's right. I shouldn't revel in this. I'm dangerous.

I concentrate until I see the thick magic tendrils wrapped around my wrists, sparkling with fire magic. I pull them back, and reluctantly, they follow my command. At least they're doing what they're supposed to do. No more burning down houses, I tell them.

When the fire sizzles out, the guys give a collective sigh. I'd join them if I wasn't worried about losing face. They don't need to know that this fire thing wasn't intentional.

"So, when are we leaving?" I ask cheerily, turning away from them so they don't see the tears pooling in my eyes.

It's hard when you realise that you're deadly.

After a quick breakfast, we're back in the car, leaving Stornoway behind. I'm sandwiched between Crispin and Arc again; the brothers have conquered the front seats. Storm is driving, as always. He's such a control freak. He'd probably die if someone else took the driver's seat.

It's nine in the morning and I feel just as tired as when I woke up. Not sure if that's got anything to do with the ritual. I tried talking to the guys about it during breakfast, but they were busy stuffing their mouths with humongous amounts of beans on toast. Arc tried to make me eat some black pudding, but I stood my ground and refused, sticking to eggs and beans instead. I'm not a vampire, I don't eat blood, no matter if it's cooked or not. Yucky.

"Guys, just to be prepared, should I be feeling any other side effects from the ritual?"

"Not likely," Crispin says, smiling reassuringly. Gods, I love that smile. It makes me all giddy and happy. Okay, maybe I am experiencing side effects. I shouldn't be fancying yet another guy.

"It might take a few days until you're able to form a mental connection with us, but with you... well, we never know."

"Yeah, I'm so special," I sigh. The boys burst out in laughter. "What? Do you know any other demi-goddesses running around?"

"Nah, and you'd be special even as a human," Arc chuckles. Aw, did he just compliment me? "A special piece of work." Oh well, it would have been too nice. I retaliate by sticking out my tongue at him. Real classy.

"So what happens if I need to contact you right now? You didn't tell me this would take days to develop."

"As I said before, two of us will be with you at all times," Storm announces. "And even once the bond is fully formed, it's just a last resort, at least one of us will need to be around..."

"No way! You told me this was a way to stop you babysitting me!"

"I never said that," he booms from the driver's seat. "And I'm responsible for your safety, so you will do what I say."

"You arrogant... dick!" Okay, not my finest swear-word-creation ever. But I'm still tired.

"It's only until we get you to your mother's palace," Frost offered quietly.

Crispin grins and pats my thigh. "Let's look at it from the positive side - when else would you get the chance to be surrounded by four hot Guardians?"

When indeed. And unfortunately, what he says is true (even though it's really arrogant). They are... delicious male specimens. I wonder if every Guardian looks like them? Probably only those created by a Goddess, I doubt Gods would like to have men around them that look better than themselves. Unless they're gay, obviously.

I yawn. "How do we get to the Realms from the Calanais Stones?"

"We activate the gate," Frost says simply. Yeah, thanks, I knew that bit.

"I mean, once we're through, are we in my mother's Realm? Or do we have to travel?"

"Gates are a little tricky. They don't always lead to the same place," Crispin explains. "It depends on the people stepping through it. If I was to go through on my own, I'd end up in my creator's Realm. Same with the other guys. But if we step through together, we can determine the destination by combining our magic and focussing on a particular place. We're hoping that it will work the same way with you."

"And if it doesn't?"

"Then we'll find another way. Don't worry, Princess, we'll get you home."

Home. I'm not sure my mother's palace will be my home. The other I had burned down, let's not forget that fact. So now I'm caught between two homes, two mothers, two fates. I'm leaving the human world behind and am entering the Realms of the Gods. It's kind of pretentious of me to think that I might be able to find a home there. I mean, I don't know anything about the Realms. I couldn't even tell you what gods they have there. Every culture has so many gods; do they all exist? Ra, Heracla, Garnesh, Quetzalcoatl, Osiris, Yahwe. Maybe my mother has tea with Loki. Who knows. Definitely not the world I'm used to.

"We're almost there, Wyn," Crispin pulls me out of my depressing musings. "I can't wait to show you the Realms. Maybe we can visit Freya together, you'll love her."

"Is she your... creator?" I ask, not quite sure whether that's a polite question to pose to a Guardian. "No, but I was... sent to as a present. Unfortunately, she rather prefers the company of women. So while she appreciated my healing skills, she wasn't interested in my other... qualities." He gives me a suggestive wink. Yeah, right. Although I guess if he was made for that purpose... My hormones are getting giddy at the thought of... No. Stop it. Enough.

"But you still visit her?"

"Oh yes, she likes to play chess, and I'm one of the few she has trouble beating." He says it without arrogance; it's a fact. I like intelligence in men. My magic purrs inside as I take in his bright blue gaze that is fixed on my face. When I look into his eyes, they grow even softer behind the blond strands of hair almost touching his lashes. Freya really missed out on something here.

Arc clears his throat behind me and I notice I am leaning towards Crispin, so close that I can feel his breath on my cheek. Oops, that wasn't intended. Stupid bond. It's turning me into a lovesick demi-goddess with no self-control and over-active hormones. Get a grip, Wyn. You're a strong, emancipated woman who is aching for her Guardi- No! Not at all.

"Please, distract me," I beg Arc as I'm trying to get my thoughts under control.

He frowns. "Is everything okay? Are you scared of the gate?"

Thanks for giving me a way out of this embarrassment. I nod. It's as good an excuse as any.

"There's nah need ta be afraid, lass. We'll be with ye all the way." He smiles at me and my insides melt. Okay, this isn't working. I can feel heat pool between my legs. Something is happening, something to do with that bond. Such a bad idea, I shouldn't have listened to the guys.

My nipples harden and strain against the fabric of my shirt. I clench my thighs together, ignoring the pulsing between them. I close my eyes and lean back against the headrest, trying to concentrate on... well, anything but my erogenous zones.

I sigh in frustration, but it comes out as a moan. Oh no. Kill me now.

"Princess, is everything alright?" Storm asks, his voice a low grumble.

"Something is happening," I whisper. "I feel strange."

"Stop the car," Crispin commands and I can feel the car come to a halt. I keep my eyes closed; looking at the guys would only increase my embarrassment. The throbbing between my thighs is getting worse and my boobs are starting to hurt.

"Are you in pain?" Crispin asks, his voice both methodical and concerned. He's having trouble staying in his healer role. I'd feel touched if I didn't already feel... well touched, physically.

"Nooooaah," my no turns into a moan. I huff in frustration. How am I going to explain without losing the final pieces of my dignity?

"I think I can feel the ritual effects," I blurt out, squeezing my eyes shut, wishing that nobody could see me. Unfortunately, I'm old enough to know that just because I can't see them, doesn't mean that they can't see me.

"Oh, that shouldn't be happening yet," Crispin murmurs.

"Well it's happening now," I screech with the full force of my upset hormones. "Do something!"

"It shouldn't be happening like this. It should start slow, over time, and then after the climax it—"

"Did you just say climax???" I scream at him, I can't help it.

"Easy, lass," Arc's deep voice booms from my right. He puts a hand on my shoulder, which immediately bursts into flames. Not real ones, but it feels like my skin is on fire. Every nerve ending is firing, sending little lightning bolts down to my core.

"Please, don't touch me," I whimper and his hand immediately disappears.

"Crisp, what do we do?" Arc bellows at his fellow Guardian.

"I don't know, none of the books speak of it happening like this..."

"Then think of something," Storm shouts, making me jump a little. The movement only makes me notice my body even more. My clothes are too tight, too restrictive. I pull at them, trying to get the shirt off my aching boobs.

"What are you - no, stop that, Wyn, you don't want to do that," Crispin yells, but I don't care.

I squirm in my seat, tugging at my clothes, trying to get rid of the heat that is enveloping my skin. I need release, now.

I hear the guys whispering around me, but I don't care, I'm too busy keeping my hands from running over my body, touching myself in all the places that matter. My self-control is standing at the edge of an abyss, ready to throw herself off to make way for her evil twin sister, carnality. Oh how easy it would be to give in. If the guys weren't here, I wouldn't care. But with them around... no. Need to stay strong.

A cool wind is blowing around me, purging some of the heat that was besieging my body. It feels good on my skin and I lean into the breeze, sighing in contentment.

"It's working!" Crispin shouts close to my ear.

I still don't trust myself to detangle my hands. They might move in the wrong direction... downwards. But the cool air is helping. A little. Enough for my mind to take back a small sliver of control. Enough not to go to pieces in front of the guys.

"Wyn, you need to tell us what's going on, we can't help you otherwise," Crispin says soothingly. I want to lean into his voice, then drag his body to me and - NO. Wrong thoughts.

I press my lips together, unwilling to even try to speak. I might moan again like a cat in heat.

"Okay, let's try a different thing. Nod or shake your head. Are you in pain?"

I shake my head. A collective relieved sigh fills the air. Oh my, I hadn't realised how worried they must have been.

"Maybe she's having a panic attack," Storm mutters, but Crispin shushes him sharply.

"Wyn, is your magic giving you trouble?"

I nod. I would have probably whimpered if I could. Pathetic. And true.

"Is it the bond?"

I hesitate, then nod again.

"Damn it, I knew we shouldn't have done that," Storm shouts and I imagine him running his hands through his dark hair like he usually does when he's angry.

"Nobody knew that it would have such a strong effect on her," Frost argues. "Otherwise we would never have done it." His voice comes closer. "You know that, Wyn, don't you? Had we known this, we would have never made you do the ritual."

I nod, hearing the truth in his words. But it doesn't help me right now. My body is still out of control, throbbing and aching and lusting for a man's touch. Or several. My magic lifts her head. Yup, that's exactly what she wants. Maybe that's the solution...

"Touch me," I whisper with clenched teeth. "Please, touch me."

Silence. Then, Crispin again. "Are you sure?"

No, I'm not. Of course not. But I nod. It can't get any worse, can it.

"We'll need to get you out of the car first," Crispin mutters soothingly. He slides one arm under my knees and the other around my back. Sparks explode where he touches me and I moan in frustration. "Not much longer," he whispers in my ear as he lifts me out of the car and sits down, with me in his lap. He lifts his voice. "Guys, come here, she needs all of us."

"Are ye serious?" Arc asks, but steps closer when Crispin snaps at him.

I'm so hot, even the cold air that is still blowing around me can no longer cool me down. You could probably fry eggs on my skin right now. Someone touches my shoulder and suddenly a burst of ice runs through me, crashing against the heat searing through my veins. Frost. Another hand, this time on my thigh, and fire and ice are pressed together in a spindling vortex. Storm. I'm feeling close to exploding with all the energy pent up in me. But something is still missing.

"Please," I whisper hoarsely, desperate for that hole in me to be filled. "Please."

Lips press against mine, bringing with them a gentle calmness that envelopes the fire, the ice, the wind, combining them, pressing them together until with a flash they turn into a ball of light, as bright as the sun and just as beautiful.

Then the ball explodes. I scream as particles of blinding light fly through my body, wild and ferocious, until they reach my heart cave where my magic is waiting for them.

She pounces and catches the light, swallowing it piece by piece until she is glowing with an ethereal shine. She licks her paws and yawns, stretching as if nothing had happened. Around her, the rainbow clouds (I still want to call them unicorn farts, but that would be immature) illuminate the walls of the cavern, making it homely and safe. I wish I could stay here, curl up like my magic, but I can hear the guys calling me. With a sigh, I leave the cave and dive up into consciousness.

"Wyn, talk to me," Crispin says frantically, shaking my shoulders.

"Stop it," I murmur, finally opening my eyes. "I'm back now."

I'm surrounded by my four guys, all still touching me (Arc's hand is now on my shoulder), all looking slightly lost. Welcome to the club.

"What the hell just happened?" Storm booms from my side. I just shake my head. I'm tired.

"Later?" I ask, and while they all look like they'd rather ask questions, they nod.

"Let's just get to that damn gate."

We're driving in silence. I'm very aware of feeling Arc and Crispin pressing against me from both sides, but it's no longer uncomfortable. No, I feel connected to them in some way, and it's reassuring to feel their bodies.

After a few minutes of looking out of the window, admiring the sparse but beautiful scenery, I ask how much longer we still have to drive.

Frost checks the map on his lap. "We should be almost there..."

We reach the top of a gentle slope and see the Standing Stones in the distance.

"Fuck."

We're not the first.

And they are waiting for us.

With an army.

Chapter Nine

Storm's face lives up to his name. His forehead scrunched, his eyes cold, his mouth a thin line, his loud breath the warning of a storm to come. He's angry; no, he's pissed.

"We need to get through there," he says through clenched teeth.

"Stating the obvious, man," Frost replies just as grimly.

We're standing on a small hill, the car behind us, looking down on the Calanais Standing Stones in the distance. And the army surrounding them.

Dozens of large stones form the shape of a Celtic cross. From what the guys have told me, an old cairn lies at the centre of the circle. That's where the Gate is.

A smoking ruin to one side of the Stones gives the scene an eerie, end-of-the-world kind of feel. Guess that may have once been the visitor centre. Until the demons arrived.

There must be at least a hundred of them. It's hard to tell from a distance, but some look more demony than others. The wings kind of give it away. Red wings, black wings, brown wings. They're not like you imagine angel wings, all fluffy with feathers; no, they're more like bat wings. This is how I envision demons to look like. For once, the stories got it right. They look evil, even from far away. Some are hunched over, walking on all fours, others are tall and upright, twice as big as your average human. I can even spot a few that have a tail. Guess now I know where humans got their image of the devil from. Some of these would make great devil impersonators, with their claws and wings and misshaped feet.

Maybe a quarter of the crowd look human, but that doesn't mean that they are. After my encounter with mages in the hotel and on the ferry (although we still don't know if that couldn't have been a Guardian), I no longer trust human-looking people. It's just me and my Guardians now. And judging from their poses, they're aching to jump into battle.

"How did they know we'd be here?" I ask (stupidly, judging from the looks my Guardians give me).

"This is the only Gate in Scotland that only goes ta the Gods' Realms," Arc sighs. "Others may get ya to the Realms of the Demons, or worse. This is the safest one... was the safest one."

"The only one in Scotland... Is there one in England?"

"Aye, doon in Cornwall, and one in Wales. We dinnae have time to travel all that way."

"So what do we do?"

Storm turns around and looks at me with determination. "We fight."

Unfortunately, I have no idea about how to use my magic to fight. True, I've managed to burn down a building and levelled a street, but those were accidents. What I need is training.

While Storm, Frost and Crispin are standing together, whispering to each other, making plans, Arc has moved away from our group and is now sitting on a boulder, his eyes closed, his shoulders relaxed. He looks peaceful at this moment. And beautiful.

"Guys, what is he doing?" I ask the remaining Guardians. Crispin comes over, putting an arm around my shoulders. My magic purrs softly inside me. His touch feels good.

"He's trying to connect with Guardians on the other side of the Gate."

"He can do that?"

"Only with Guardians who have the same telepathic ability that he has. There aren't many of those, though, so it would be rather lucky. But even so, there is a telepath living in your mother's palace, so he will be able to pass on a message to her majesty."

"Will she be able to send help?"

"To her side of the Gate, yes. But she won't be able to send her forces to earth. She made that law herself, so even if she wanted, she couldn't break it." He notices my confused look. "The laws she enforces are magic. If someone breaks them, it has severe consequences. And as the creator of the laws, it would likely kill her."

Oh. Well, guess we're on our own.

I look down at the demon army again. They're not doing much; most are sitting around the stones, waiting. Waiting for us.

"Can we do it? Can we fight them?"

Crispin sighs and squeezes my shoulder. "I'm not sure. Just us four Guardians? No. We might be able to deal with half of them, but in the end, they'd overwhelm us. But you? You're a wild card, we don't know what you can do."

I laugh, slightly hysterically. "Neither do I."

"Which is why we're going to train you," Storm's booming voice interrupts. "We need to see what you're capable of. We've seen your raw power, but it now needs to be shaped into a weapon."

He pauses, looking down at me with something resembling sympathy.

"It wasn't supposed to be like this, Princess. We shouldn't have to force you to explore your magic before you're ready. But the longer we stay here, the harder it will be to break through their ranks. We'll train for a day. Hopefully, that will be enough. If not... it'll have to be enough."

He turns and goes back to his brother, who has spread a map of the island out on the bonnet, staring at it in deep thought.

"Are you ok?" Crispin whispers, his arm still around my shoulders. I lean against him, needing his touch. For a moment, he doesn't react. Maybe I've gone too far. Maybe he meant it just as a friendly gesture. Nothing more than a friend-

He turns me around until I'm looking into his bright-blue eyes. He lifts his hands and gently touches my cheek. With one finger, he touches the sensitive skin under my eye. I want to fill the space between us, but with his other hand he keeps us apart, pressing against my shoulder. He's confusing me. His touch is so gentle, so full of meaning, but at the same time, he's not letting me get close.

He smiles softly and sighs. "Not here," he whispers and turns away, leaving me on my own. I can still feel the ghost of his fingers on my cheek.

"Chesca!" Arc shouts suddenly and jumps up from the boulder he sat on.

A collective groan comes from the guys behind me.

"No, not her. Isn't there someone else?" Frost mutters.

"Who's Chesca?" I ask, already a little apprehensive. This can't be good.

The guys look at each other uncomfortably.

"She's the lover of a fellow Guardian," Frost finally says. "She's got a cottage not far from here where we can stay and train."

"Okay, that doesn't sound so bad."

Arc cringes. "She's also a demon."

"Wait, aren't all demons supposed to be evil?"

"Yeah, usually they are. But Chesca is... well, she's got her moments..."

"She's trying to be good," Frost explains. "But she isn't always successful in that."

"Why is she trying to... oh, because she's in love with a Guardian?"

"Aye. She really must love him to fight her nature. You'll understand it when you meet her. She'll cheat you and trick you, but in general, she can be trusted."

"Sounds like quite a piece of work," I muse. "This will be the first time I'll meet a demon."

"After that, you'll meet them on the battlefield," Storm says tonelessly. I had him down as someone revelling in the chance to fight some demons, but somehow, he looks... sad. Regretful. Not defeated, though. And that's the most important thing.

"Arc, what did the Guardians say?" Storm addresses the Scot.

"There are aboot ten waiting on the other side of the Gate, including a healer. Beira has been informed. Not much more they can do."

"Then it's up to us. Let's go, there's no time to waste."

We follow Storm back to the car. Time to meet Chesca.

The cottage looks like it's been taken straight from a fairy tale. White-washed walls, a thatched roof, potted flowers under the windows, a wooden bench next to the green door. I decide that one day I want to have a cottage just like it. Maybe a bit bigger so my Guardians can all fit in it.

It takes me a moment until I notice what I just thought. I included the guys in my plans for the future. That can't be right. I've known them for all of three days. That's not enough time to fall in love. But here I am, dreaming of a cottage with my men. Could I get them to do the dishes? Yes, that's me, immediately thinking of the practical side of things.

Before we can even get out of the car, the green door opens and out steps a... well, I guess she's a demon. But she's unlike the demons I saw at the Calanais Stones. This demon is beautiful, in an evil, demony kind of way. Her wings are golden with black tips, and she seems to have pierced the upper edges of them and decorated them with a row of golden rings. A golden tail is wrapped around her hips, but somehow, she pulls it off and makes it look elegant. Nothing but a tiny black dress covers her golden skin; one of those dresses that would make most women look desperate. Not her though.

She's taller than your usual human woman; slim and perfectly formed. Her boobs are a little smaller than mine though, I notice with relief. Not sure why I compare her to me. Maybe it's the way she hungrily eyes my Guardians. That's right, *my* Guardians.

She's striding towards the car, hips swaying from side to side (including her tail), wings opened to show off her impressive span. I only now notice that my mouth is wide open and I'm openly staring at her. Well, excuse me, this is my first demonic encounter.

Storm gets out first, walking away from us to meet her. The other guys look on, apparently reluctant to leave the car.

"Are all female demons like her?" I whisper.

"She's one of a kind," Crispin sighs. "We better follow Storm or he might try to kill her."

"Any particular reason for that?" I ask innocently. Not that I'm jealous or anything.

"Before she fell in love with Aodh, she was... well, she was very interested in Storm. She got a little stalky. He didn't like it."

"But she doesn't think about him like that anymore, right? She doesn't fancy him anymore?"

"She's a demon, Princess. She fancies everyone."

"Oh. Everyone?"

"Aye, she'd have you for breakfast if she could," Arc laughs.

"In a sexy or cannibalistic way?" I ask carefully.

"Both, if you let her."

"I'm not sure I want to meet her."

They just laugh and get out of the car. Thanks a lot, bringing me to stay with a questionable demon before making me fight against other demons. Demons seem to be taking over my life. And Guardians.

"So, this is the sweet princess I've heard so much about," Chesca whines in a sultry but rather annoying voice.

I lift an eyebrow. "You have?"

Her innocent smile turns into a snarl. "No, sweetie, I have not. And I don't care who you are." Her features smoothen again. "Please come in, I've got some lemonade in the fridge."

She turns, almost hitting me with her tail, and saunters back into the house, beckoning us to follow her. I look at the guys who are all in various poses of suppressed laughter.

"Is she always this... changeable?"

"Oh lassie, that was nothing," Arc grins. "Wait until she starts arguing with ya. She actually switches between supporting and opposing ya."

"Sounds like fun. Shall we?"

I leave them behind, their snickers following me into the cottage. It's pretty inside; furniture in white and light browns make it look bright and comfortable. Not like I imagine the home of a demon to look like at all. I wonder what her bedroom looks like. Black? Iron chains hanging from the ceiling?

Chesca is waiting for us in the kitchen, holding two glasses of lemonade. She offers me one, I stretch out my hand to take it and - she lets it drop to the floor. Cold lemonade drenches my feet. "Ooops, I'm so sorry, dear," she smiles at me with a fake wink. "But I'm sure with your magic you'll be able to clean it up?"

Before I can even say anything, the lemonade lifts off the floor (and my shoes) in a large, yellow bubble and hovers over to the sink. I look behind only to see Frost lazily wave his hands around.

Chesca hisses. "I wanted her to do it!"

"Well, I did it instead, so deal with it," Frost replies calmly, his hands in his pockets.

The demon's expression changes from angry to seductive. "Oh, I'd like to deal with you, sweet Guardian. Will you guard me tonight?"

"Come on, Chesca, you can do better," he laughs.

"I can indeed. Why don't you let me show you? Upstairs." Her voice is a sultry sexiness that makes my knees wobble, and she didn't even talk to me. This demon is oozing sensuality.

"Cut the crap," Storm growls, "we're not here for your little games."

"Oh, but you are," she purrs, "you just don't know it yet." In a flash, she's standing next to Storm, her tail wrapped around his waist. She presses her perfectly formed body against his chest and -

Without thinking, I act. On my command, the jug of lemonade lifts from the kitchen table and flies through the air until it's hovering straight above Chesca's head. I smile and give my magic a nudge. The jug topples, releasing the lovely, sticky lemonade.

The demon shrieks and jumps away from Storm. Mission accomplished. He's mine, bitch.

With a hateful glance at me, she storms out of the room.

I look at my Guardians, who seem a little shocked. I grin and they start to laugh, until we're all bent over, giggling together about a lemonade-covered demon. Even Storm. I know, it's a miracle.

When we've recovered from our laughing fits (it takes Frost the longest to be able to keep a straight face), we sit down at the kitchen table.

"Demons are weakest at noon," Crispin begins, surprising me. I thought Storm would tell us what to do, as usual. "That means we have about twenty-four hours to train you, Wyn, and get ourselves ready for battle. I propose you train one-on-one with each of us. Three sessions today, one early tomorrow morning. That should give you enough time to recover and have your full energy to fight."

"Sounds good," Storm says, surprising me again. Since when does he let other people make the decisions?

"I agree," I barge in, not wanting them to make all the decisions. "Who will I train with first? And what are you actually going to teach me? I mean, I know that Storm can play with air and Frost with water—"

"I like her," Chesca interrupts, standing in the doorway. "She's talking to you with just the right mixture of patronisation and sincerity."

We all gape at her. How can one person...ehm, demon... be so changeable? Leaning against the doorframe, she arches her back slightly, presenting her full breasts and tiny waist. Such a poser.

"But I think I could teach her some things, too," she continues, ignoring our stares. "Things that you Guardians may be too prude to teach. Things that she will need once she enters the Realms. Gods can be such schemers."

Storm clears his throat. "That's very kind of you, Chesca, but for now Wyn has to prepare for battle. We need to get through the Stones as soon as possible, and will worry about court intrigues later."

"Spoilsport." She actually sticks out her tongue at him. I giggle, earning me a hateful glance from her. I'm almost relieved that she's behaving like a demon again, not like a sultry succubus.

She turns to leave, but then whispers, almost like an afterthought, "If you want to know what Storm likes in bed, come find me."

I choke on my own spittle and Crispin has to slap my back a few times until I can breathe again. How dare she...

"Aaaanyway," Frost laughs," let's go back to your training. As you so eloquently put it, I *play* with water. Storm's talent is air, Crispin's is healing and Arc specialises in the manipulation of the mind. We know you also have some fire and earth magic, so Crispin will test what you can do with those."

"We don't know if you have any healing powers," Crispin explains, "and we won't have time to use them in battle anyway. I have studied all the magic abilities known to us, so I'll be able to help you more than the other guys."

I nod. "When do we start?"

"That's the spirit, lass," Arc booms. "And ye'll start with me."

Chapter Ten

I meet Arc outside, behind the house. There's not much around the little cottage: bare, low hills, moorlands, and in the distance, the sea. It's beautiful in a very simple way. I take a deep breath, enjoying the tingle of the salt air in my nostrils. I could get used to this view. Everything is so quiet here. After living in the city all my life, this is very different. Good different.

I wonder what the Realms will be like. I imagine them looking like something out of a fairy tale, with a touch of middle ages thrown in. No electricity, no streets, no cars. But maybe I'm totally wrong about that. I mean, there's magic, right? Who says magic can't power a house. Maybe they've even got internet over there.

Well, first I have to get through those Stones, then I'll be able to find out.

Arc is standing with his back to me. His kilt is moving gently in the breeze, as is his ginger hair. His broad shoulders are relaxed as he looks into the distance. He's gorgeous, in a rugged, hard sort of way. Not as hard as Storm though, who is the master of grimness.

I run towards him and jump up, hugging him from behind. My magic purrs inside me. Yes, I admit, satisfying the bond between me and the guys feels nice. Too nice, almost.

"Lass, good to see ya," Arc says with his deep voice, smiling.

I rub my hands, looking at him expectantly. "How do we start?" If I didn't have as much self-control, I'd be jumping up and down from excitement. I'm finally going to explore my magic!

"How much do ye know about what I can do?"

"Ehm, I know you can change memories; you did that to my neighbours after I... well, after my magic exploded. But that's pretty much all I know."

He sighs. "I dinnae like meddling with people's minds. Too much can go wrong, too much ta mess up. But sometimes I have nae choice. But I can do other things. Reading people's mind ta tell if they're lying."

"Oh, I can do that," I interrupt.

"Ye can?" His bushy eyebrows arch in surprise.

"I've always been able to. Only with humans though, I think. At least I can't do it with you guys."

"That's cause we're shielded. Maybe ye can try with Chesca later on. Demons are quite similar ta humans in this matter. Most mages are shielded. Gods cannae be read at all."

He smiles. "One less thing ta teach ya. What ye really need ta learn though is how ta shield yer own mind. Some demons can take control of mages if they dinnae shield enough. And I dinnae want ta imagine what a demon possessing ya could do..."

I shiver. No, neither do I. And thinking back to when those mages kidnapped me, I realise how important this shielding is.

"How do I do it?" He smiles at my enthusiasm. Arc seems very smiley today. I hope it lasts. I love his dimples.

"Let's sit down." He motions me to a group of boulders. Good thinking; the ground is far too squishy and wet to sit on.

When I'm seated on a stone opposite him, he begins his explanation.

"Close yer eyes. Relax yer body. Focus on yer limbs. Are they relaxed? Let go of any tension ya feel. Now, breathe in - hold - and breathe oot." I feel like he's turning into some kind of yogi. His usual deep voice has softened, taking on a calm, peaceful tone. I could listen to him for hours.

I follow his instructions, breathing deeply, focusing on how my breath expands my rib cage and then deflates it again.

"Now, imagine an island. It doesn't have ta be big, it could be just a small piece of sand in the middle of the ocean. Imagine sitting on this island, just like ye're sitting now. Ye're relaxed. Listen ta the sound of the waves. Listen how they become louder, wilder. They're turning into a storm. Ya have ta protect yourself from the elements. Imagine a dome of glass, covering your entire island. It doesn't have to be high, but it needs ta touch the ground everywhere. There cannae be holes, no places for the water to enter."

I'm feeling a bit like Robinson Crusoe, sitting on my tiny island under a palm tree. It's hard to focus; my belly is full of butterflies that flutter with every word Arc is saying. That bond will be the end of me.

I need to focus.

Taking another deep breath, I imagine a dome, and when I breathe out, I drop it on top of my island. It almost crushes me, but it's just high enough so I can stand up. Apparently, I can destroy things even in my imagination. I really need to get to grips with all this magic stuff.

"Do you have that dome?" Arc asks, his voice soft and gentle.

I nod, trying not to lose focus.

"Good. Now let's test how strong it is. I'm going to try and break it. Don't worry, I'm not going to hurt ye."

I steel myself against his coming onslaught, thinking he'll try to crush the flimsy dome I have erected around me. Instead, nothing happens. The waves continue to beat against the glass, but no more than before.

I relax a little. Maybe my dome is strong enough to withstand Arc's powers? I'm a demi-goddess after all, maybe my powers are stronger than those of a Guardian.

I smile - and shriek as I suddenly notice Arc sitting next to me on the sand.

He frowns at me. "Ya failed. Let's try again."

He disappears into thin air, leaving me shocked and disappointed into myself. Pride comes before the fall, etcetera.

I shake off the feelings of rejection, and focus on my dome again. I look for any holes or cracks he might have used to enter. And yes, there's a large cleft at the bottom of the dome where water is slowly pouring through. Damn it, Wyn. Focus. This is no game, even if there's a hot Guardian involved.

This time, I make sure there are no cracks. My dome is smooth and strong.

"Still not good enough," Arc rips me from my jubilations. He's sprawled out on the sand next to me, taking in the view. Waves are crashing against the glass, some even manage to roll over the dome completely.

"What did I do wrong this time?" I whinge. "I thought I had everything covered."

"Did ya think of what happens underwater?"

I huff. No, I didn't.

"So, it's not supposed to be a dome, but a sphere? Why didn't you say so?"

"Because then I couldnae have done this." He pulls me against himself and crashes his lips on mine. I know this isn't real, I know this is just happening in my mind, but it *feels* real. I part my lips slightly, and Arc takes that as an invitation to nudge them open further, entering my mouth with his tongue. We merge, our mouths pressed together, our minds entangled. It feels beautiful. His lips are soft and firm against my own, his hands are gripping my hair, pulling me even closer against him. With a final touch of his tongue against my own, his lips leave my mouth, travelling downwards, leaving kisses on my chin, then my throat. I moan and lean back into his arms that are holding me in place. I close my eyes, revelling in the feeling of his hot breath on my skin. His tongue is trailing lower, drawing circles on the nape of my neck. I moan softly and in response, he gently bites my skin.

"Open yer eyes," he whispers hoarsely. When I do, his mouth descends on mine again, giving me a heated kiss, before breaking apart. I'm breathless, waiting for him to come back, to touch me again, more, everywhere.

He smiles. "Look down."

I do and - holy fuck, my shirt has gone! I'm naked, from the waist up; no bra, no shirt, just my bare skin. He grins. "And this is why you shouldnae let me into yer mind."

Before I can protest, his mouth is on my right breast, suckling on my nipple. Why would I ever protest against that? I lean back, his hands still holding - I fall into the sand.

He's gone.

I'm alone on my island, lying in the sand, half-naked.

"Aaaaarc!" I scream in anger and frustration. He didn't even have the decency to leave my shirt with me. There's nothing to cover me with. Not even a giant palm leaf I could use, Eve-style. I growl. That man is going to be killed slowly. Maybe I'll even ask Chesca to help me. I'm sure she'd love a good Guardian torture followed by a Guardian roasting. Or dismemberment. Yes, that's a good idea. Totally going for dismemberment.

"Get ready, I'll try again," Arc's voice comes from far away.

I'll show the bastard. He's not getting in here again. My magic moans in disappointment. Shush, girl. Pride over pleasure.

I extend my dome downwards until the edges meet. I glue them together, forming a perfect sphere. No one can enter now, not even from below. Not even Arc. I pour all my energy into the glass, making it stronger, unbreakable.

He is not going to best me again.

Every muscle tight and ready to act, I wait. No surprises this time, no matter how pleasant they may be.

I look out into the waves still crashing against my sphere. The sea is boiling, dark waters are fighting for dominance. Is that... yes, there's someone out there, in the water.

A large body, naked, fighting against the waves.

Arc.

He reaches my protective orb, his fists pummelling the glass. His face is desperate, he's trying to speak but that would mean he'd open his mouth to the water. He'd drown. He's scratching the glass, trying to get a grip on it. I run to him, placing my hands against the glass. His eyes meet mine, wild and full of fear. He's drowning. I need to help him.

I concentrate. I built this sphere; I can break it. With as much force as I can muster, I slam my fist against the glass, breaking it.

The dome collapses.

Water enters, quickly overwhelming me. Arc has disappeared. It's just me, the waves, and my last breath.

I open my eyes with a gasp. The first thing I do is check whether I'm dressed. I am, thank the Gods.

Arc is watching me from the stone he's sitting on.

"You shouldnae have done that," he says sadly. "No matter what ye see in your mind, ye can never let down your barriers. Understand?"

"But you were drowning," I splutter.

"It wasn't real. Demons will show ya all kinds of things ta trick ya."

I nod, embarrassed. I failed his test. Damn it. Why does that affect me so much? Why do I care so much what he thinks of me?

"Come on, let's try it with the others. Keep your barrier up, alright?"

I nod, still a little downtrodden.

"Don't look so sad, lass. Nobody expects ya to be perfect from the start."

"But I need to be able to do this tomorrow, Arc," I argue. "I don't have the time to practice again and again."

"Aye, I ken. That's why we're practicing with Chesca."

I gulp. Maybe I'm not so keen now.

I follow Arc back to the cottage. The other three Guardians are sitting in the kitchen, having tea and what looks like scones. Someone else has joined them, a man, just as beautiful as them. I assume that's the Guardian Chesca is trying to be good (or better, less evil) for.

He gets up when we enter the room and does a half bow.

"Princess, it's an honour to meet you."

I smile, unsure of what to do. I promise myself that one of the first things I'll do in the Realms is to learn basic demi-goddess etiquette.

"The honour is mine," I reply, remembering a line I've heard before in fantasy films. All that binge watching is finally coming in handy.

"Wyn, this is Aodh, a fellow Guardian," Storm introduces the man. "He is Chesca's..."

"Fiancé," Chesca interrupts from behind us. She squeezes past, managing to rub her bum against Arc. Damn that demon. She slides onto Aodh's lap. "We got engaged last month."

"Congratulations," Storm sighs.

Arc leans down and whispers into my ear. "They get engaged every few weeks, then split up again. We're no longer taking it very seriously, and I doubt Aodh is."

Aodh smiles patiently. "Would you like some tea, Princess?"

I nod. "And please call me Wyn. I don't feel like a princess yet."

"That will come," he says sagely. "You'll grow into your role once you've spent some time in the palace."

"If we ever make it there," I mumble while reaching for a scone. They look delicious. I wonder if Chesca made them. Somehow, I can't imagine her standing in the kitchen, cooking and baking. But then, what do I know about demons. Maybe they're quite domesticated.

I smirk and take a bite. Okay, it was definitely Chesca who made them. They're disgusting. I think she used salt rather than sugar, and added a hefty dose of vinegar. I've never eaten anything so rancid.

The guys look at me expectantly. Only now I see that they haven't touched their own scones. Thanks for the warning.

I swallow with determination, then smile at Chesca. "They are delicious, did you make them?" She nods, her expression brightening. "Yes, do you like them?"

"Words fail me," I reply, trying to keep a straight face. Frost is hiding his face in his tea cup, trying not to burst out laughing. The other guys aren't faring much better; all are looking slightly choked. Even Aodh seems to be having trouble not to grin.

Oblivious, Chesca beams at me. "Do take another, sweetheart, I've got more in the living room."

Please kill me now.

Luckily, Arc comes to my rescue.

"I'm afraid we don't have much time. I've taught Wyn how to shield her mind, but she needs practice. Chesca, would you mind..."

Still smiling widely, Chesca nods graciously. "Of course. Darling, look at me."

I only realise that she's talking to me when Storm pointedly clears his throat.

"Ehm, yes." I shift in my seat until I'm facing her.

"Is your barrier still up?" Arc whispers. I quickly check on my little island, and see with relief that a new sphere has formed around it. I give him a quick nod and he smiles at me reassuringly.

Chesca leans forward, while still being sprawled out in her fiancé's lap.

"Close your eyes, pumpkin." I almost choke, but manage to do as she says. Again, I find myself on my island. The sea has calmed a little, but it's still rough out there.

Slowly, a mist rises from the water, gathering around the edges of my sanctuary. From the mists, a woman appears. Chesca. Her wings are stretched out wide and she's as naked as she was on the day she was born (or created, or crawled out of hell; whatever demons do to start their life). She gives me a seductive little wave. Well, seductive perhaps if I was into women. Or into demons. But instead of looking at her little sultry display, I think of my Guardians. All four of them, together, surrounding me, like on the ferry, but this time Crispin has joined the others. I breathe in their scent, their masculinity.

Chesca has no chance against the force of my vivid imagination.

Her features change from seductive to angry. She claws at my glass sphere, and while it shakes slightly, it holds. No cracks this time. Take that, demon bitch.

W hen I open my eyes, an angry demon is looking at me. But I'm more interested in the proud looks my Guardians are giving me. I passed the test. Yay me.

Chapter Eleven

I follow Frost outside. We're not staying close to the cottage this time; instead, we're following a well-trod path leading to a tiny loch. More of a big pond, really, surrounded by heather bushes.

"I thought it would be easier to practice with a small pool of water rather than going to the sea," Frost smirks and I smile gratefully. I have no idea what to do with water. On my birthday, it was ice and snow that attacked me. Is that the same as water magic?

"To manipulate water, you first need to understand the essence of water."

I frown. "That sounds very philosophical."

Frost laughs. "You might like this bit. Undress."

"What?!" Not again. These boys are driving me crazy with their attempts at getting me to go nude.

He sighs. "You can leave your underwear on. You could even leave all your clothes on, but then you'd be dripping wet afterwards, and I can't have you get ill on the day before the battle."

He's got a point. But I'm not going to concede that easily. "But it's cold… It's not like it's summer," I moan.

He just smiles patiently. "Touch the water."

I give him a confused look but bend down and put a finger into the water lapping at the shore of the loch. I laugh in surprise. It's warm! Perfect bathing temperature, actually.

"Now, get undressed, we're going for a swim." True to his word, Frost pulls his shirt over his head, exposing his sculpted abs. Gorgeous. He catches me staring. I blush and turn my gaze away. No need to show him how much he affects me.

When he slides down his jeans, I busy myself with my own clothes. I really don't want to do this, but then… yes, I do want to. Before I can change my mind, I strip down to my underwear and run into the water, almost slipping on the muddy ground.

The water is quite murky, which is good because it hides my body from Frost's heated eyes. Yes, his gaze is following me, his expression hungry. He's still wearing boxers, but now he's putting his hands on the waistband and pulling them down - I turn away, staring at the water that has suddenly become very interesting. Fascinating. So much better to look at the water than at his… bits. Although I'm sure they're impressive. Gah, no. The water is impressive. Exactly.

"You can turn around now," he laughs, very aware of my embarrassment. I slowly turn, making sure that it is indeed safe to look. He's standing in the water, wading towards me. It's like the water is parting way in front of him, making him appear a lot more graceful than I must have looked when I walked into the loch.

I'm standing on muddy ground and I don't even want to imagine what creatures might be looking at my toes just now. Or what creatures I'm standing on. Yucky. I should really learn how to walk on water like Frost did when he rescued me from the sea. But then, I'd be half naked. Okay, maybe not.

"Now that you're surrounded by water, it will be easier for you to reach for its essence," Frost begins his lesson. "Water is fluid, slippery, and not easy to control. It's much easier to simply go with its flow, and gently manipulate it to change direction, rather than force it to do your bidding. But for now, I want you to simply observe. Don't try to control the water, just watch and learn from it."

"Makes sense."

He smiles. "Good. Close your eyes and don't open them until I say so."

I do as he says and concentrate on my surroundings. Water is gently lapping around my shoulders; tiny waves are breaking on my collarbones. Below the surface, I can feel the different temperatures of the water - it's colder towards the ground, but still warm enough not to feel cold. Whatever Frost has done to heat up the loch, I want to learn.

My hands are floating in the water, weightless. I sway a little from side to side, giving way to the slight current.

From the way the water moves, I can feel that Frost is coming closer.

"Now extend your magic. Reach into the water, explore it. Don't try to change it though. Just see what happens."

That's strange. I've never used my magic to explore something. Usually I just throw it out there, lighting a candle (or a house) or opening my curtains. This is new. I'm amazed that I've never thought of doing this before. But then, nobody has ever bothered to teach me (yes, mother, I'm talking to you).

Keeping my eyes closed, I extend a few magic tendrils from my fingers. At first, I don't feel anything besides my own magic, but then... it's hard to describe, but it's like my magic is being gently pulled from side to side. Just like a leaf bobbing on water, I guess. Just that usually, nothing can affect my magic. This is new.

It's not a strong pull, more like a playful movement, as if the water is testing how far it can go. This is weird, I'm talking about the water like it's intelligent, like it knows what it's doing.

"Do you feel something?" Frost asks, his voice close to my ear.

"Yes, the water is somehow moving my magic." It's hard to find words for this strange feeling.

"That's fantastic! I didn't think you'd be able to feel it this quickly. Now, use your magic to draw some water into yourself."

Ehm, how am I supposed to do that? My magic is invisible, but water is solid - well, fluid, but you know what I mean. But I trust in Frost's water knowledge. Let's do this.

I imagine one of the magic tendrils floating in the water as a straw, then gently suck on. In my mind, not for real. Although I can't help my mouth making a slight sucking sound.

Slowly, water is being pulled in by my magic; a dark blue string wrapped around my magic tendril. It feels cool as it enters me, but not wet, strangely enough. But then, this is not my body feeling things, it's my mind. My magic.

The water magic is different from my own; they don't mix. But now that it's inside me, I can control it. I form it into a little ball, just big enough to fit into my hand. Then I push it out, just like I would with my own magic.

I open my eyes. True enough, there's a ball of water hovering over my hand - but it's rather large. Twice as big as me, in fact. Oops, apparently, I underestimated my strength.

Frost is snickering behind me. "Bit overambitious today?"

I laugh with him. "Today? Always."

I admire my water sphere. I can't believe I actually created that. And it didn't take a lot of energy at all. Maybe water magic is my strongest power.

"Now release it, slowly," Frost says, still laughing.

Oh yes, I will. With an evil grin, I move the water until it's straight above Frost and let it fall. It crashes down on him. And on me. Apparently, I'm not good at estimating distances. That backfired (backwatered?). Oh well, at least the water is still fairly warm. Could have been worse.

I think, and am suddenly pushed down, under the surface. Once I'm fully submerged, Frost's hands disappear from my shoulders and I resurface, spluttering obscenities. Bastard.

I turn around and glare at my Guardian. Revenge will be sweet. Wet, actually.

It doesn't take much effort to summon some water magic into me and expel it as a massive burst that hits Frost in the chest and throws him backwards. Gotcha!

He's pushed underwater and disappears.

And doesn't resurface.

Oh oh.

I may have just killed my Guardian.

The water around me suddenly turns cold. Very cold. I wouldn't be surprised if it turned into ice, it's that freezing.

"Frost!" I shout, already beginning to shiver.

"What are you going to do now, little Princess?" His joyous voice is at odds with the anger I feel as I see him walking towards me. He's walking on water again. Like freaking Jesus. A very naked Jesus.

"Make it warm again!" I growl, shooting him a hateful glance.

He just laughs. "Do it yourself." And turns, and walks away.

Son of a bitchy mermaid!

Okay, what do I do now? How do I make it warm? Asking the water magic nicely? Threatening it? Nah, there needs to be a better way of doing it. What generates heat? Movement.

I take as much of my magic as I dare and throw it into the water, shaking it from side to side, swirling it through the icy water. The water doesn't actually move, but I can see its essence slowly changing colour. And temperature. I sigh in relief.

"Crude, but effective," Frost comments from behind me. How does he always manage to sneak up on me like that? Granted, I was busy wasting all my magic on heating an entire (small) lake.

"Now, don't let go of your magic but pull it back in. The temperature won't change, don't worry."

I follow his advice. Thank the Gods, it works, otherwise I wouldn't have been much use in my next lessons. A demi-goddess without magic is worse than a human.

"Well done," he grins at me, sitting down on the water as if it was a solid surface.

"How do I do that?" I ask hungrily. This skill will totally make me feel like a proper deity.

"You just have to believe that you can," he says simply.

"Thanks for that extensive explanation," I snarl.

"You're welcome." He extends a hand and I grip it. A second later, I'm in his arms, standing on the water next to him. Cool. Then he lets go of me, and I fall back into the water.

"Believe."

"You do know you sound like some crazy preacher?"

He smiles. "I believe in you. Guess that makes me a believer in the divine Wynter."

I gape at him. "I'm not divine."

"Aren't all Gods?"

"Yeah, but I'm not a God."

"Sweetie, you just managed to heat an entire lake. Only Gods and Guardians can do that."

Okay, I admit, I'm speechless. And a little proud.

He pulls me out of the water again. He uses so much force that I stumble against him - and I don't really stop. He catches me in his arms and presses me close. That's when I notice that I'm in my wet underwear. And he is naked. Oh, so naked. And apparently, he's noticed the same thing. Instead of releasing me, he hugs me even closer. His hard cock presses against my stomach. I don't mind, strangely enough. My nipples are just as hard - but that's from being wet in the cold Scottish air. And not that kind of wet. I mean, dripping. Nooo. Lake water-wet. That's it. He's not affecting me in the slightest.

"Wyn," he whispers, and I melt into him. I look up, and my lips part in anticipation of meeting his.

His kiss is soft and gentle; so different from the demanding kiss of his twin. But it feels just as good. He tastes like the sea, salty and cool at the same time, and I want to savour more of that taste, so I plunge my tongue into his mouth. He moans and runs a hand through my hair, gently guiding my head so I look up at him. His soft brown eyes stare into mine while our tongues dance, and I can see his desire burning in them. I'm sure mine look just the same. I want him. I need him.

I run my hands over his back, feeling the hard muscles around his shoulder blades. He nibbles on my bottom lip, and in surprise, I claw at his back, my fingernails leaving marks on his skin. He moans again and it makes me even needier. My Guardians have been teasing me for so long - first Storm, then Arc, now Frost. I need more than just their kisses.

So, I go in for the kill. I grab his arse with both hands and squeeze, pulling his pelvis against me, rubbing his hard cock against my belly.

"Wyn," he gasps, pulling back from my lips for a moment. I wait for him to say something, but he only continues to breathe heavily. Well, he had his chance. I stand up on my toes and kiss him. He sighs against my mouth, then returns the kiss, hungrily. He's more forceful now than before; the sweet kiss has turned into a victorious conquest.

I run my hands over his back again. I need his touch. I need to feel him.

He pulls back, but only for a moment, then gently presses my shoulders, motioning me to the ground - well, the water's surface. I still can't believe we're standing (making out) on top of a loch. But I don't have time to ponder, as he pushes me down until I'm lying on my back, looking up at him. He kneels by my side, running his hands over my belly, then higher, until he reaches my breasts. He kneads them through the wet bra I'm still wearing.

"Take it off," I whisper hoarsely, and he complies, carelessly pushing it up until my boobs are exposed.

"You're beautiful, Wyn," he groans, and leans down, taking my left nipple in his mouth. He uses his hands to gently squeeze the other one, running circles around my puckered areola. I moan and arch my back. No idea how he manages to get me to this point just by kissing, but I feel so close to coming already. My skin is hot and I am desperate for release. He's teasing me, but I need more. I grip his head with both hands, pulling him off my breast and pushing him downwards.

He chuckles. "I was going to get to that, Princess."

"I need you now," I groan. "Please."

His tongue traces a line on my skin. When he reaches my belly button, he nibbles on it. I almost laugh, but it turns into a moan. I push him further. Stupid Guardian. He's not getting the message.

I'm getting hotter - and I mean my temperature. I can feel sweat pooling on my forehead. No other man has ever made me feel this way. I'm desperate for a drink, but I'm even more desperate to feel Frost, all of him.

His tongue has finally reached its destination. Almost. So close. But he teases me, licking too high, not in the right spot. And he knows it.

"Frost!" I shout, ignoring how needy I sound.

He chuckles, then finally presses his tongue against my core. I cry out, and so does he.

But while my cry is in pleasure, his is in pain.

"Stop, Wyn, stop it!"

I sit up and gasp in shock. A circle of flames surrounds us, violently fighting against the water barrier Frost is throwing up against it. Sparks are exploding all around us.

He turns and I can see his back, the skin an angry red where the fire burned him. I panic.

"I don't know how to stop it!" I cry, wringing my hands at the chaos I have caused.

"Pull back your magic!" Frost shouts back, throwing his arms in the air, summoning a wave that crashes against the wall of fire. But it's not enough to quench the fire.

Get a grip, Wyn. You can't let him get hurt even more.

I concentrate until I can see my magic, flaring angrily all around me. I've never seen it so violent. I try to pull it back, but it doesn't react. My usual magic tendrils have turned into a raging inferno that's totally out of my control.

"Stop it at the source!" Frost calls desperately, throwing more water at the fire.

I close my eyes and search for my heart cave inside. It's burning; the cave is filled with flames. My magic is snarling at me angrily; she's telling me it's not her fault. I ignore her and pull in some water magic like Frost taught me earlier. I pour it in into the cave, more and more, until it extinguishes the flames. From my Guardian's relieved sigh, I know that the fire around us has also been extinguished.

My magic shakes her dripping fur, shoots me an evil look and turns, licking her wounds.

Which reminds me...

"Frost, how bad are you hurt?" I run to where he is kneeling on the ground, his shoulders slumping with exhaustion.

"It's okay, Princess, I've had worse."

"It's not okay, my magic hurt you. I hurt you." I sink down next to him, examining his back. It's bad. Burns are covering most of the skin, ranging from bright red to blistering.

"We need to get you to Crispin," I whisper, my heart turning cold in shame. This is all my fault.

I help him up, pulling one of his arms over my shoulders, and together we make our way back to the cottage.

Him, burnt and naked. Me, miserable, guilty, in my underwear.

Chapter Twelve

W hat have you done now," Crispin huffs.

"It wasn't me," Frost protests, but Crispin just raises an eyebrow and ushers us inside the cottage.

Aodh and Chesca are sitting in the living room, but get up when they see us. The Guardian motions us to the sofa. "You can lie down there, Frost."

Chesca mutters something about blood stains, but one look from her Guardian lover silences her. Wow, I hadn't realised just how much influence he had on the demon diva.

With a groan, Frost sinks onto the sofa. Crispin stands next to him, moving his hands through the air above Frost's burned back. I can see him weaving a net of thin magic strands, delicate and beautiful.

"This is your first lesson in healing," Crispin mutters, his forehead scrunched in concentration.

"I hadn't planned it to be like this," I reply sadly.

"Don't worry, Princess," Frost calls, his voice muffled from between two pillows his head is lying on. "I'm happy to be a lab rat for you."

"Ehm... thanks. You're making me feel so much better."

He laughs, then groans as Crispin lowers the woven-magic-net onto his back.

"Magic by nature is without purpose," Crispin explains while manipulating the web. "Only the magic user's intention turns it into a tool. When I wove this net, it was just a shape, nothing more. Just energy assembled in a certain way. Now, though, I'm putting intention into it. I'm telling it to take on a purpose and heal Frost's injuries. You need to give it precise instructions. It's easy if it's something like 'light a candle', but with healing, you need to tell it exactly what to do. Which is why medical knowledge is essential even for a magic healer. I need to know what the skin needs to be healed. Does it need fluids, blood, chemicals to mend itself."

"So even though I have magic and could weave a web like yours, I wouldn't actually be able to use it to heal?" I ask, a little confused. This sounds so unlike the magic I normally use.

"You may be able to heal a broken bone, but you likely wouldn't be able to repair the injured tissue around the break. Once we're in the Realms, I'm going to teach you the basics so you can heal at least minor injuries yourself."

Frost snickers. "What he's basically saying is that this is a lesson in how you know nothing and how he can't teach you just now."

In response, Crispin flicks a finger and a part of this magic net presses down on Frost's skin. He wails.

"What were you saying, my friend?"

"Nothing. Only that you're the best healer ever. Now could you please get on with it?"

Crispin sighs. "As you wish."

With practised movements, he waves his hands through the air, his fingers manipulating the magic like a spider tugging on her web. Some of the magic strands flow into Frost's body, others spread out on his skin. Slowly, I can see them having an effect. His flesh looks less red, and the blisters shrink until they disappear completely. Within minutes, Frost's back is as flawless as it was before the... accident.

With a final shake of his hands - think maestro conducting the final notes in a symphony - Crispin lets the magic dissipate and steps back from his patient.

"Now, would someone please tell me how Frost ended up burned while teaching you water magic?"

The other Guardians have joined us in the living room to listen to my sorry tale. It's the most embarrassing story I've ever had to tell. I set the man I was going to have sex with on fire.

Yeah, I'm sure that happens to everyone at some point in their lives. Not.

When I finish, there's silence. Even Chesca is quietly staring at the floor. It's making me realise just how bad this is.

"You said you felt hot just before it happened," Aodh finally says thoughtfully.

"Of course she felt hot. Just look at him," his lover giggles. "If I had those muscly arms touching me, I'd be hot as well."

I blush. In fact, my face has been red throughout this whole conversation. They all wanted to hear a lot of detail... Embarrassing.

"Maybe it was just because her magic hasn't settled yet," Storm suggests. "She's not had time to properly explore what she's capable of."

"It doesn't sound like a normal flare," Crispin replies. "No, she said her magic was under attack - right, Wyn?"

"I don't know if that's the right word for it. My cave," Frost snickers at that word for some reason, "was on fire, just like everything around us. But I don't know what happened first."

"Aodh, you're the expert in fire magic," Storm says. "Have you ever heard of this happening?"

The Guardian shakes his head. "Not that I can remember. I'll have a look through my books though, maybe I can find something."

"Good. Arc will help you. Frost, you need to sleep, the healing will have used up a lot of your energy. Crispin, it's your turn to teach Wyn. But this time, I'm staying with you. If something like this happens again, I don't want you to be on your own."

I'm about to protest, saying that being with Crispin doesn't mean I'm on my own, but one look at Storm's stern face shuts me up. I know a lost fight when I see it.

I sigh. "Okay then, what do we do?"

Instead of going outside like I did with Arc and Frost, Crispin takes us upstairs, into one of the bedrooms. I'm beginning to love this cottage more and more. Everything is so tastefully decorated, quaint and cute. I'd imagine a little old woman to live here, not a demon diva. I'm totally going to call her that from now on. It fits.

We sit down on the thick rug that covers most of the floor in front of a four-poster-bed. Storm stands in the door, watching. He's making me nervous. With him here, I feel it's like a self-fulfilling prophecy, a magic accident waiting to happen.

"Would you please sit down," I say tensely when he still doesn't move. He huffs and moves across the room, sitting down on the bed. He's just as tense as I am; poised to jump up and intervene. I hope that won't be necessary.

"Wyn, we don't have much time," Crispin interrupts my worried thoughts. "You've had your lessons with Arc and Frost, do you think you learned enough to use those elements tomorrow?"

I think about that for a second. Despite the mishaps and disappointments, I have learned something. Hell, I managed to throw Frost across half the lake. And I kept Chesca out of my head - something I'm enormously grateful for. I feel like I've only begun to scratch the surface of what I could do if I had more time, but there isn't any. We still don't know who tried to kill me, and the longer we stay here, the easier it will be for them to find us. We need to get through the Stones, demon army or not.

"Yes, I think the water will come in handy. Although, I've only used water magic while actually standing in the loch. How do I summon it while being on dry land?"

Storm sighs and I cringe. I can feel his disappointment prickle on my skin.

"Frost taught you to connect to the water's essence, to recognise it. Now that you've done that, it's easy. Stretch out your magic just now. There's water all around you, in the air, in the ground, in the pipes. If you pull strong enough, it will come."

I stretch out my awareness and notice he's right. I see the world around me differently now. It's like I've developed a new sense - faint, but still there. I know that there's a pipe just below my right foot; I know that there's a little stream about fifty yards away from the cottage. I can even feel the water in the Guardians' blood around me.

My surprise must have been visible on my face, because Crispin gives me a wide smile. "You got it?"

I nod, returning the smile. Finally, success.

"Won't it take a lot of energy though to summon water all the way from the stream?"

"Not if you give it some leeway. Can you feel in what direction the water is flowing?"

"Yes, away from here, towards the sea."

"Good. If you were to summon water from the sea to you, it would be against its flow, against its nature, so you would need a lot of energy. But if you take it from the other direction, it's already flowing towards you, so you only speed it up a little. Doesn't take much force to do that."

"Makes sense." I think back to the water I felt around me. "Silly question, but can I get water from blood?"

"No," Storm thunders, making me jump a little. "Never, ever manipulate the magic within other beings unless you want to harm them."

"Of course I wouldn't want to harm you, but what about the demons? Couldn't I like... I don't know, make their blood boil or something?"

Storm opens his mouth to say something, but Crispin is quicker. "It's a valid question, Wyn. One reason we don't do that is because most people don't have enough control to only affect the blood in one demon. They might injure or even kill their comrades." He sighs. "It's one of the few ways Guardians can be killed."

"Oh." That shuts me up - for a few seconds, at least. "But if you had the control, wouldn't it make sense—"

"You've proven earlier that you do not have the control, so stop arguing," Storm shouts, getting up from the bed. I gape at him, but then nod. He's right. And it was his brother who I burned, so it makes sense that he's angry. But still, why does it hurt so much to see the anger on his face? Anger that's directed at me?

"Storm, take a moment," Crispin admonishes his fellow Guardian. "Go outside, Wyn needs to concentrate."

Storm gives him an annoyed look, but leaves the room, leaving us alone. Only now do I notice that my eyes are a little wet. Oh Wyn, why are these men making you behave like a hormonal cry-baby?

"He doesn't mean it, Wyn," Crispin says softly. "What you asked... he lost a friend that way. It's not a pretty way to die. When you've seen it once... well, you'll only use that method when there's no other choice."

"I understand," I whisper, mortified at what Storm must have thought of me.

Me, behaving like the murderer of his friend.

"I know you do," Crispin smiles. "Which is why I know you would have asked many other questions, am I right? We just chose to focus on the wrong one."

I frown. "But how am I supposed to fight if I don't know anything? A day isn't enough to prepare. Am I just supposed to drop a ball of water on those demons? All Arc taught me is how to shield my mind. That won't help me when a demon is standing in front of me, trying to kill me. I need tools, weapons, something quick that will help us get through to the Stones without getting killed."

"And that," Crispin is still smiling, "is why you're here now. You know I'm a healer, but knowing how to mend a body also means knowing how to break one."

Understanding grows in me. And sadness at the thought of Crispin, this innocent, funny, helpful Guardian having to use his healing magic in such a way. It's wrong. And despite his smile, his clenched fists tell me that there is a story here. One I'm not sure I want to hear.

I've always known that there was more to Crispin than his cheery exterior. But now that I may be close to finding out more about it, and I'm pretty sure I don't actually want to.

"There are many ways people die." Crispin's voice has turned cold; his face an emotionless mask. How did he change so quickly?

"Their heart stops, their breathing stops, their organs fail, their brain stops sending signals. So many different ways we can cease to exist. Even Guardians can die under the right circumstances." He pauses for a moment and I don't dare to speak.

"And so can demons," he continues with determination. "They can be killed, and I can teach you how."

I'm not sure I want to anymore. Not that I ever wanted to, really. I've never killed anyone in my life. In fact, I rescue spiders and put them outside before my mother finds and kills them with a fly swat. I'm that non-killing. And those demons haven't threatened me yet, have they? All they're doing is standing around the Standing Stones. Maybe they won't even stop us?

"Don't lie to yourself," Crispin sighs. I stare at him in shock, then look inside me, scrambling for my barrier. It's down. He read my thoughts.

"Why did you do that?"

"Because you need to learn. You need to learn to keep your mind shielded, you need to learn to fight, you need to learn not to hesitate when a demon stands in front of you, ready to kill you. We need you to get through this alive. So, I'm going to teach you. It has to be done."

Now he's beginning to scare me. Not in a he's-going-to-jump-me kind of way, no, in a he's-hurting-himself-by-helping-me way.

"Take my hand." When I hesitate, he reaches over and clasps my fingers with his. "Now, send some of your magic into me. Not into my mind, into my body."

"What if I hurt you?"

"You won't," he says with such confidence that I close my eyes and send a single magic tendril through our clasped hands.

When it flows into him, I get the strangest sensation. I guess this might be what amputees experience when they feel their limbs even when they are no longer there. It's like a have a second body, but it's fleeting, like an echo of something that once was. I pour a bit more magic into it and the awareness of this other body becomes stronger.

"Can you feel my toes?"

Without even having to think, I know that I can. There they are, comfortably warm in his socks. I nod, fearing that speaking might break my concentration.

"Can you feel how I'm sitting on the floor?"

Yes, I notice how his bum touches the uneven rug. Ehm, strange feeling. For a second, I debate to try and see how some nearby body parts feel like - this might be the only chance ever to explore the male anatomy from this perspective - but I refrain from doing so.

"Can you feel my heart beating?"

With a single thought, I'm up there in his chest, feeling every contraction of his heart.

This is so strange. I can see his heart contract, no, it's more a kind of feeling rather than seeing it. And somehow, I know that if I reached out and touched it, I could make it stop.

I pull back into my own body in a flash.

"Why did you let me do that? I could have hurt you," I accuse Crispin.

"I knew you wouldn't. But you need to know how you could do it."

"So how is that better than, you know, boiling your blood?"

"It's quick. It's almost painless. And if you don't want anyone to know... people die from heart attacks all the time."

My eyes widen. He's no longer talking about killing in battle. He's talking about assassinations.

"Now, let's try it without me touching you."

He leans back, his hand leaving mine. It's cold where I miss his touch. I concentrate and send some magic his way. Entering his body is made more difficult without the physical contact, but it's still fairly easy. Just a small push and I'm in. This time, I go straight to his heart, marvelling at how this small thing manages to power his entire body. I want to reach out, touch it, take away the pain that I know is hiding somewhere inside - but that would be foolish.

I leave Crispin's body and return to my own.

Only to find that something is wrong. I can't quite put my finger on it, but there's this strange feeling in my throat, like some food got stuck there. I swallow, but the feeling isn't going away. In fact, it's getting stronger; my airways I slowly closing.

"Crispin," I gasp, but my Guardian is sitting still, his eyes closed. "I can't breathe!"

His brow furrows, but the pressure around my windpipe is increasing. I wheeze, trying to get as much air in as possible.

"Cris..." My voice fails. Black spots are dancing in front of my eyes and I can feel myself sway, even though I'm sitting on the ground. In a desperate move, I open my mind, removing the barrier, shouting out for help.

Not that I expect anyone to hear me.

My last breath leaves me.

I can't breathe any longer.

I slowly sink backwards, but I barely feel my head touching the floor.

"Release her," Storm's thundering voice drifts through my foggy mind.

"I can't, she'll kill her," Crispin mutters.

"She's gone. She can't hurt them. Now let her go!"

A slap echoes through the room. My throat opens and I gasp for air.

"Wyn, are you okay?" Frost is by my side, helping me sit up. I'm woozy and lean against him for support. What the hell did just happen?

Slowly my vision returns to normal.

Crispin is staring at me, wide eyed. There's nothing but fear in his turquoise eyes, a panic that must be unbearable.

"Arc, take him outside," Storm commands, and the big Guardian lifts up Crispin, who is totally unresponsive, and drags him out of the room.

Frost is gently stroking my hair while Storm is looking down at us, his expression more emotional than I have ever seen it.

"I shouldn't have left you two alone," he finally says under his breath.

"You didn't know he would still be affected like this," Frost says soothingly, still running his fingers through my hair.

"What just happened?" I ask, my voice hoarse and crackly.

Frost sighs. "Crispin has... issues. When he was created, it wasn't to have a protector or even lover. No, his Goddess fashioned him to help her in other ways. She thought she could create a tool who would blindly follow her twisted wishes. But Guardians have an intrinsic sense of right and wrong. Even then, at the beginning, Crispin knew that what she asked of him was wrong. So, his Goddess made him a sister. He must have really loved her, cause he started to do what was asked of him. I don't know all the details, but according to the stories she turned him into an assassin. An inquisitor."

"He did some terrible things," Storm mutters.

Frost waits for a moment, then continues. "When Beira heard about it, she intervened. But the Goddess didn't give up easily. Somehow, Crispin's sister died. He doesn't talk about it, but it broke him. Beira sent him to Freya, to start a new life. It took him a long time to recover."

"Apparently, he's not recovered yet." Storm's voice is a duet of sadness and anger.

My heart breaks for Crispin.

"What was her name? The Goddess who created him?"

The twins stay silent for a moment. Then, Storm clears his throat.

"She is the Morrigan."

Chapter Thirteen

I wake with a feeling of dread burrowing deep within my stomach. There is no gentle awakening, no remaining dreaminess. No, I know straight away: today we're going to have to fight. And if this goes awry, there may not be another morning for me and my Guardians.

For the hundredth time, I am asking myself if we really have to do this. We could just hide out somewhere on Earth, waiting for our mysterious pursuers to give up. Apparently, the Guardians have access to quite a bit of money; surely, they could afford a flight to an exotic island somewhere.

But Arc was right last night when he argued that this demon horde wouldn't stay by the Stones forever. They would get hungry and would take to the nearby villages. People would get killed.

We need to get rid of them, and travel through the Gate in the process. Preferably with all our limbs intact.

I sit up, looking around the room. My Guardians are camped out on mattresses on the floor; after last night, they all felt they needed to be close to me. It's cute, in a way, but I wish that it wasn't because Crispin was suffering from a homicidal case of post-traumatic stress disorder.

It had been a very quiet evening. The absence of our usual banter and laughter made me go to bed straight after dinner, and the guys followed quickly after. We hadn't talked much about what had happened. The twins refused to tell me more about Crispin's story. And Crispin was in no state to talk about it - and I wouldn't have asked him anyway. If he ever decided he was ready, he probably would. For now, he had to deal with the guilt of almost killing me.

I didn't blame him, but he wouldn't listen. He had sat in a corner, not meeting my eyes, not speaking, hardly even reacting when one of us addressed him.

I search for him in the dim room. His mattress is empty, the duvet neatly folded on top.

The other guys are still sleeping - okay, ignore that, Storm is awake, watching me from his place close to the door. His face is hidden in shadows, but I can see tiny specs of light reflect on his open eyes. I sigh and get up. Storm lifts his head.

"Where are you going?"

"Looking for Crispin," I whisper.

For a moment, I think he's going to stop me from leaving, but then he throws his blanket back (his abs look even more chiselled in the dark) and gets up as well. He puts on a shirt that's lying in a heap on the floor next to his mattress, but he doesn't do up the buttons, giving me a full view of his muscular body. Did I mention he's only wearing boxers?

Well, if he wants to play it that way... I'll stay in my pyjama top and shorts. Not that I've got a body like him, but maybe it's enough to make him just a tiny bit uncomfortable.

He opens the door. It creaks and Arc lifts his head, but when he sees that Storm is with me, he lies back down again.

Good. I don't need them all to come with me.

I follow Storm through the quiet house. The first light of the morning is illuminating the rooms just enough that we don't need to switch on the lights to find our way.

"Where are we going?" I whisper.

"I know where he is," Storm replies simply, and I don't ask any more questions.

When we reach the main door, I regret my choice of clothing. I hadn't thought that far ahead. It will be freezing outside.

But if I go back to our room now, Storm might just go to Crispin on his own. I sigh and slip into my shoes. There's a coat rack in a corner, and I randomly choose a jacket - judging from the slightly perfumed smell, I assume it belongs to Chesca.

Storm only put on his boots, not taking a coat. He still hasn't buttoned up his shirt. Yeah, real manly. Show-off.

When he opens the door, an icy wind welcomes us. Looks like autumn is slowly turning into winter.

The sun is rising over the hills in the distance. It looks like it's going to be a beautiful day.

I step outside and breathe in the crisp air, trying not to think that this may be my last sunrise.

My last chance to talk to Crispin.

Storm walks around the house and follows the same path to the loch that I took with Frost yesterday afternoon. He's quiet; all I hear are our footsteps on the slightly frosted ground and some birds singing their morning songs.

By the time we reach the loch, I'm freezing. Not putting on proper clothes was such a bad idea. Storm halts at the banks of the lake and turns around, taking in my shivering form.

He shoots me a wolfish grin (yes, he can smile!). "Maybe we should turn this into our first lesson."

Suddenly, the air around me begins to warm. My shivering stops and I move my arms through the hot air, soaking in the warmth. Just when I've almost reached the perfect temperature, the air turns cold again.

I give Storm a scornful look. He shrugs in response.

"Your turn."

"How do I do this?"

"Frost said you know how to heat water. It's pretty much the same thing."

"Shouldn't we look for Crispin instead?"

"Don't worry, we will in a moment. We're close."

His reassuring voice calms my worries a little.

Okay, let's do this. I close my eyes - I find this makes it a lot easier to reach my magic - and feel for my heart cave. My magic is snoring softly but perks up when she notices that I need her. She yawns and I have to smile as she stretches her glittering body.

I send out some magic tendrils and begin to weave them together. No use in doing it with single ones; I'm hoping this will be quicker. I managed to warm the water by swirling my magic through it, and I'm hoping it'll be just the same with air.

When my net is finished, I grip it tightly and mentally throw it around, swinging it like a lasso all around my body. Enough movement will hopefully make it warm in no time.

Already I can feel a slight change in temperature. Then a breeze grasps my hair, quickly turning into something more forceful. Wind begins to howl around me and I open my eyes.

Shit.

I'm standing inside a wind hose which is circling me faster and faster. Storm has retreated to a safe distance, but instead of helping me he's bent over laughing. The wind is too loud to hear him, but it looks like he's roaring with laughter. Bastard. Little help, please?

I pull back my magic, but the wind doesn't stop. It's now moving on its own volition. I sigh in exasperation. I'm such a terrible mage. I wanted to make the air warm and instead I created a tornado. I guess this skill could come in handy in battle though.

I'm still in the eye of the storm, but it's slowly moving. If I step out of the calm centre, I'll be thrown through the air. Not sure if it's worth the risk.

"How do I make it stop?" I shout.

At least Storm has the decency to stop laughing. He steps forward, waving his hands in the air. Just like that, the wind dissipates.

That looked way too easy.

He gives me a mock bow, then grins. "You may want to work on your technique, Princess."

"My technique?!" I huff. "You didn't teach me how to actually do this!"

"He's not the best teacher," a low voice chimes in from behind us. Crispin!

He's walking towards us, his face expressionless. Gone is the smile I fell in lo- ehm, that I've grown to like. His hair is messy, but not the intentional messy he usually achieves with half a bottle of hair spray. His clothes are torn in places, and small twigs and leaves are stuck to his jeans.

In summary, he looks dreadful.

Well, at least we found him. Or, he found us.

"What were you doing?" I ask, giving him a quizzical look.

He looks down on himself, only now seeming to notice the state of his clothes.

"Oh... I went for a run," he mumbles.

"And nature got in the way?"

"Yeah, something like that." His voice is missing its usually chime. I almost want him to shut up, just so I don't have to hear this empty, different Crispin.

I don't know what to say, and apparently, neither do the guys. I look out over the water; it's smooth as a mirror this morning, with only a few leaves breaking its surface. If I had the time, if this was a holiday rather than a battle preparation camp, I'd go for a swim.

But no, I've got other priorities. Like staying alive.

I sigh. "Storm, what did I do wrong earlier?"

"You forgot that the air doesn't give as much resistance as water. You put in too much force, too much magic. The air needed to get rid of that excess energy, so it turned into a shape that lets it do that."

"Seriously? Couldn't it have become something less threatening than a tornado?"

He laughs, surprising me.

"Try it again. This time, make your magic smaller, thinner. You don't need to start a storm, you just want to shake the air a little. Imagine shaking a sieve to get all the water out. That's the movement you mentally need to make."

I nod. "You better stand back, I don't want to hurt you."

They do as I say. Pity, I would have liked them to protest, only to summon some wind to push them back.

This time, I leave my eyes open. I don't want to be surprised by a tornado again. I try to take just as much magic as I need, then spread it out in a thin mesh all around me. I give it a gentle shake, like a sieve.

My hips become warm. It worked! Well, in a way. I should have probably wrapped the mesh all around me instead of having me in the centre of it like a tutu skirt.

I gently move my magic while continuing to make it vibrate. Warm air surrounds me. Bingo.

Storm and Crispin come closer, now that they see I won't kill them with a little hurricane. I extend my magic mesh (that should become a brand name one day) until it wraps around them.

Storm gives me another smile. Wow, he's really cheery today.

"Well done. See, it wasn't hard." His smile turns devilish. "To practice, you should see if you can change more than one air temperature at the same time. How about you make the air around Crispin a little colder?"

A second later, Storm shouts obscenities.

"Oops, did I confuse you two? Sorry, I didn't mean to make the air *that* cold."

In response, Storm stretches out one arm and pulls it back immediately. Something grabs me around the waist and throws me forward, into Storm's waiting arms.

"That's cheating!" I complain, fighting to get out of his grip. He just laughs, making his chest vibrate against my own.

"It's all part of our lesson. Now try and escape, using just your wind magic."

"And you won't defend yourself with your own?"

"No, I won't."

It's hard to concentrate when you have a muscly Guardian press against you. And a bond inside your heart whispering how lovely it would be too raise my head, pull his lips towards me, use my other hand to... Gods, one day this bond is going to get me killed. I need to practise.

How do I get out of his grip with wind without injuring myself? He's holding me tight; even if I used the same trick as he did on me and pulled him back with an air-lasso, he wouldn't let go of me. Somehow, I need to make his hands move away from my upper arms.

I weave some little magic tendrils and knot them around his fingers. Now, how do I add some wind? I try the straw technique, but apparently, you can't do that with air like you can with water. Next, I *wish* the air to do something. Well, guess it was worth a try.

If all that isn't working, maybe the painful method will... I wrap an air lasso around his waist and one around mine and pull them in opposite directions. My legs are pulled off the floor until I'm flying almost parallel to the ground. Storm is fighting against the wind, but even his feet are almost lifted up. But he's not letting me go. I will the air to pull more - and I slip out of Storm's arms, but he grasps my wrists, keeping a hold of me. Dammit. I'm a bit afraid of what will happen when he lets go. I'm not sure if I can stop the pull at the same time as making sure I don't crash to the ground. But it doesn't matter, I need to win this challenge.

I ask my magic and with a satisfied purr she gives me access to all her reserves. I pour the magic into the wind, making it stronger, wilder. Storm is lifted into the air; we must look like skydivers just now, floating in the air with outstretched arms, holding onto each other.

Well, him holding onto me.

"Let go," I hiss, but he just smiles at me.

"I am not responsible for what happens now," I growl, and begin to spin us in a circle. Maybe if he gets sick he'll let go.

But then I have a much better idea. He's going to hate it.

I stop us spinning, and focus on his trousers. To be precise, his boxers. It's not my fault he's not wearing anything else. With a grin, I grip them tightly with some bands of air, and pull them down. He shouts and let's go of my hands, covering his modesty. We're pulled away from each other by the air lassos I have still wrapped around our waists, but I manage to let them guide us to the ground. We actually manage to land without too many bruises.

Crispin begins to laugh as he sees Storm tumble to the ground with his boxers hanging around his ankles.

The sound of his laughter is an even better feeling than the knowledge that I just managed to best Storm.

Together, we head back to the house. After grumbling at me for what felt like hours, Storm had shown me a few more handy wind tricks. But I know it won't be enough for battling a horde of demons.

Outside the cottage, Chesca and Aodh are sitting on a bench together. The Guardian has an arm wrapped around the demon's shoulders, and she's positively purring as she's snuggled against him. Here's a sight I never expected to see in my life.

Aodh looks up when we approach and untangles himself from his fiancée.

"Storm. Crispin. Princess. We've decided to join you today."

I gape at him, waiting for Storm to protest, but my Guardian simply walks towards them and clasps arms with Aodh.

"I am grateful, brother."

"We wouldn't be able to sit here, knowing that you were fighting a horde of demons." He gives Chesca a pointed look and she hurries to nod and make some agreeing noises.

I guess it wasn't her idea.

"When do we leave?"

"Let's be ready by eleven, that gives us time to have breakfast and prepare."

I look at my watch. Two more hours until we might all die. And Storm is talking about breakfast.

Men.

Chapter Fourteen

I t feels surreal, stepping out of the cottage, ready for battle. Five Guardians, one demon and one demi-goddess. The guys have donned armour that Aodh had stashed somewhere, and all of them have some kind of sword (I don't know anything about weapons, so all I can say is that Storm has a long big one, Frost two short ones, Crispin's looks more like a large dagger, and Arc has the biggest of them all). They've given me a dagger which I've got in a sheath strapped around my waist. Not that I'd know what to do with it. All I've cut in the past have been vegetables.

Chesca is wearing a crop top and cargo trousers. And me, I'm in my normal clothes, with the addition of a stab vest. Now I just have to tell the demons that they can only attack me on my torso.

Standing in a line outside, I feel like we're superheroes. The Seven Avengers. Something like that. We split up into two cars; our own and Chesca's Ferrari. It's pink, by the way.

I'm feeling queasy and hope I won't have to ask the guys to stop en route so I can throw up. I still have no idea about what I'm going to do. The Guardians have come up with a plan, and I know my role, but that's not the same as actually being prepared to use my magic to kill.

"It'll be alright, lass," Arc whispers and puts an arm around my shoulders. I lean against him, savouring his touch. I will never forgive myself if something happens to my men.

Down to earth, funny Arc. Cheeky, helpful Frost. Brooding, strong Storm. And gentle, damaged Crispin.

My Guardians.

When I focus on my magic, I can feel my bond to them. It will help me later on if I need to know where they are. That will be one of my roles: telling them if one of the others is in trouble. They will always know where I am. Finally, this bond will come in handy.

I snuggle against Arc. From my other side, Crispin grabs my hand and presses it reassuringly. I smile at him and he gives me tense smile back. He's not returned to his normal self yet, but at least he's talking again. When all this is over, I need to have a long chat with him.

The drive is over far too soon. We're back at the crest of the small hill from which we can see the Standing Stones. The demon army has grown since yesterday. It's hard to tell, but I'd say there are at least 150 demons in all shapes and sizes lazing around the Stones.

Our chance of success has just shrunk even further.

We get out of the car and wait for Aodh and Chesca to join us. They're walking arm in arm, and my heart warms at seeing their love for each other. It's strange to see a demon behave this way, while a horde of her brothers and sisters are waiting to kill us.

"You all know what to do?" Storm asks, his voice all business.

Everybody nods. There's no point in talking anymore about this. We've discussed our plan often enough. Now we just need to put it into practice.

"Wyn, test your bond one last time."

I sigh, but focus on the invisible tether that binds me to my Guardians. This morning, Aodh showed me how I can tug on it to get their attention. I could talk to them, but that would mean opening my mental barriers, which would be too dangerous. Instead, we're sticking to these simple tugs. If one of my Guardians feel it, they need to return to me because either myself or one of the others are in trouble. Easy.

I give them each a gentle pull, and one after the other they shudder. Apparently, it's a rather strange feeling.

"Good. Aodh, Chesca, are you sure you want to do this? You can still return. No hard feelings."

"Don't offend us, brother," Aodh says quietly.

"Yes, let's kill those monsters," Chesca adds cheerily.

I don't tell her that theoretically, she's the same species as them.

"Would you give us a moment?" Storm asks the couple, and they retreat back to their car. Chesca wraps her golden wings around her fiancée and shields them from view. Handy trick for making out in public.

I'm left with my Guardians. I look at them all, unsure of what to say. Who knows if we'll all be alive by the end of this. In silence, we stand in a circle, listening to the seagulls riding on the wind above us.

Finally, Frost steps forward, taking me in his arms.

"Group hug!"

With a grumbling laugh, Arc joins him, hugging me from behind. Without hesitation, Storm and Crispin follow, until I'm squeezed in the middle of my four Guardians. For a moment, I feel safe.

Then they step back and take their warmth with them.

It's time to fight.

The plan is to split up: Frost will circle the demons to reach the sea, Storm will accompany him about half way there and then find a good spot to stay, Arc and Chesca will circle them from the other side, and Aodh approaches them from the front. Crispin and I stay close to the burning visitor centre, where we can see the battlefield but are not directly part of it.

Crispin needs to be protected so he can heal the others when necessary, while I will join the fighting later. With my magic being so unpredictable, I'd probably just destroy the well thought out tactic Storm and Crispin have devised.

Still, I feel left out. I don't want to kill, but I also don't want to stay behind when everybody else is fighting. I'm supposed to be the most powerful one, for fuck's sake.

But my Guardians have made a compelling argument. I'm the only one who can connect to them all. If one of them gets injured, I'll try and get Crispin to them without him getting injured. Crispin may have killed in the past, but he's not like the other three. He's more of an assassin than a warrior.

So, while the other three are fighting with swords, our weapons of choice are binoculars.

There are no goodbyes. The others just leave, some of them nodding, some of them smiling. Storm only gives me one final look, then turns away and doesn't look back.

"It'll be alright, Princess," Crispin murmurs. "This isn't our first battle."

"Have you ever been this outnumbered, though?"

"No," he admits. "But with Chesca and Aodh on our side, and you, of course, we have a much better chance. We'll get you to that Gate, Wyn. Soon, you'll finally step foot into the Realms. Tonight, we might already be feasting in your mother's halls."

"She actually has 'halls'? Plural?"

He smirks. "Yeah, the palace is rather large. There's the Great Hall, and then there are smaller ones for different functions. Her throne room is pretty impressive. There are some simpler rooms as well, of course, but your mother has had a long time to build and decorate the palace. It's a piece of art."

"I can't wait to see it."

I guess I can't wait to see my mother, either. It's been years. She won't have changed, she's looked the same for thousands of years, apparently. But I have, both physically and mentally. I'm going to have to ask her some uncomfortable questions. I need to know, finally, why she's been absent my entire life. Why she never prepared me for moments like these - battles, abductions, meeting a psychotic demon.

First things first, though. We've got a battle to win.

Something tugs on my magic. Arc. That means he's in position. Two more to go. Frost has the longest way, but the closer he is to the sea, the stronger his magic.

Another tug. Storm.

Aodh won't be able to tell me when he's in his agreed place, but he's the closest one and we should be able to see him. Although he's warned us that he's an expert in camouflage. As a fire mage, he's got access to smoke that can hide him - add a smoking visitor centre and it's the perfect camouflage.

Finally, the third tug. Frost has reached the beach.

One Guardian at each point of the cross the Standing Stones form. We're ready.

"They're in position," I tell Crispin. "Are you ready?"

"Not much I can do to prepare. All I do is wait for someone to get injured. I can imagine nicer pastimes."

Yeah, I didn't think about that.

I look into myself, finding my heart cave. My magic is alert, looking ready for battle. Good girl. I tug at the bonds connecting me to my Guardians. Crispin wheezes next to me.

"Sorry, it's easier when I pull at them all at once," I apologise.

"It's okay. Guess I'll get used to it eventually."

In silence, we watch the demons lazing around the stones. They've posted a few guards on their perimeters, but most of them aren't paying attention to their surroundings. They're relying on their numbers to be enough of a deterrent.

Well, we've got no choice but to fight.

And we will beat them.

Suddenly, a fire erupts at the bottom of the cross, close to the visitor centre. Almost at the same time, a wall of water rolls over the beach, at least ten feet high; while a small tornado springs into action to the right of the Stones.

The battle has begun.

Chapter Fifteen

My Guardians kill dozens of surprised demons before the rest of the horde notice that they're under attack. Smoke is rising from the battle line closest to us where Aodh is conjuring a wall of fire that slowly pushes forwards. It's drifting towards us and the smell of burned demon fills my nose. It's probably the most disgusting thing I've ever smelled.

In the distance, balls of ice are raining down from the sky, carried through the air by gusts Storm is creating. On the other side of the battlefield, several demons have begun to attack their own ranks. That must be Arc's doing.

It's chaos, but that's exactly what we want. This isn't about killing as many demons as possible just now. It's about identifying which demons are the strong ones, the ones we need to look out for.

During breakfast, the guys gave me a crash course in demonology. Apparently, some of them have almost no magic, they purely rely on their physical powers. That doesn't mean that their claws, beaks and teeth aren't any less deadly than magic. Then there are the ones who specialise in different elements, just like mages and Guardians. Most of them only have one power, and are physically weak. The problematic ones are the higher demons, who have several magical skills and physical prowess. Usually, they are the leaders, more intelligent and devious than their fellow demons. In the worst cases, they're like corrupted Guardians, equal in strength and intelligence. Our hope is that none of those, or only a few, are at Calanais today.

Storm's theory is that the higher demons won't join the fray immediately. Which is why Crispin and I are now searching the battlefield for potential demon leaders. I press the binocular against my eyes, trying to see as much as possible.

There's one standing perched on top of a fallen stone close to the centre of the circle. His bright-red wings are outstretched and he is shouting at the demons on the ground below. Black horns erupt from his forehead, almost looking like a stag's X. A bushy mane runs down his spine to where a long tail grows from just above his arse. I point at him and Crispin nods.

"A fiend. I had hoped there wouldn't be any. They're the princes of the Demon Realms; strong and unpredictable. See the barb on his tail? It's poisonous, deadly to humans and debilitating to Guardians. Let's not find out what it does to demi-gods."

He points to the entrance to the cairn, which is now guarded by a giant, fleshy demon. It looks a bit like an orc that's been boiled in hot water. Not pretty.

"I think I know her—"

"Wait, that thing is a woman?"

"I've not had a chance to check her anatomy," Crispin says drily. "But her name is definitely female. They call her Brenda. She's got quite the reputation. She likes to kill her victims slowly and brutally. She's also partial to nibbling on them while they're still alive."

I shudder. "Can we kill her?"

"With pleasure."

We spot two more higher demons: one that looks almost human, except that his skin is bright blue, and another who seems to be a cross between a yeti and... well, something with four arms.

I regret that it's not my task to kill those demons. At least, not yet.

The Guardians have managed to turn the area around the Stones into chaos. Demons are running around screaming, some are lying on the ground, dead or injured, and the higher demons are barking commands.

But now that the initial attack has passed, the demons are starting to fight back. A group of them has separated from the horde and is running down to the beach, apparently trying to circle Frost, who has moved away from the sea to be closer to the battle line. If they succeed, he'll be surrounded. If only I could use my bond to send him a warning - but both his and my own mind need to stay shielded. We don't know yet how strong some of these demons are. Possession doesn't sound like much fun (not that they can actually possess you like in the films. Instead, they break your mind and control you, turning you into a mindless slave. But because that shell of a human talks what the demon wants it to, it looks like possession).

"Crispin, they're trying to—"

I was worrying about nothing. Frost has turned around and an icy blizzard is now surrounding the demons who tried to sneak up on him. I almost want to cheer him on, but that might make the demons aware of our position. It's not like we're hiding, but we're far enough away from the battlefield to not draw attention. Hopefully.

Crispin laughs grimly. "Look, Storm's using your techniques now!"

A tornado is surrounding Storm. It looks a lot more planned than the one I conjured by accident in this morning's lesson though. Gods, was that really just a few hours ago? It feels like years have passed.

Demons are trying to get to Storm, but instead, they're lifted off their feet and thrown through the air. Impressive.

I look over to the other side of the Stones, where Arc and Chesca started their attack. I can't see them. "Crispin, where is Arc?"

He scours the battlefield with me. They've disappeared. "Where could they have gone?" I ask, worry hugging my heart.

"They must be around somewhere... They're going after one of the higher demons, so they must be cloaked - ah, see there, behind that blue wobble demon?"

I swallow a question about the 'wobble demon'. It looks exactly like it sounds. Imagine a blob of jelly that has a head, arms and something that looks like stocky legs. And it's bright blue.

Behind it, a golden demon has appeared, ignored by the other demons around it. Despite her colouring, Chesca blends in. She drags Arc behind her, shouting something to the wobble demon. He turns around and inspects my Guardian, who is looking dazed and not quite right.

Anger bubbles up in me. "Chesca! I knew she was up to something!"

Crispin chuckles. "Wait, I don't think it's as it seems."

The blue demon stretches out an arm to touch Arc - and the arm flies through the air, cut off by Arc's sword. A second later, that same sword has buried itself in the demon's chest. I shudder as the demon... dissolves. Yucky.

Chesca holds up a hand to high-five. That's her, high-fiving on a battlefield. Crazy.

"One higher demon less to go," Crispin murmurs next to me.

"How many are there?" "I've counted six so far, but that's only those who are physically strong. There may be some that look unremarkable but are higher demons nonetheless."

"So they're outnumbering us."

"Princess, have you counted the demons? They've outnumbered us from the beginning."

I huff. Of course I knew that. But there's a difference between having 150 stupid demons or 144 stupid demons and 6 very strong ones.

Crispin gasps and points to where Frost is fighting.

"He needs help!"

My Water Guardian is surrounded. More demons must have followed the initial breakaways. He's shooting icicles in all directions, but whenever a demon goes down, another takes his place.

I reach for my bond and give Storm a tug. I can see how he falters for a moment and know my message got to him. Now he knows someone is in trouble. Once again, I regret that I can't give him more information via the bond.

But he's already running towards his brother, blowing demons out of his way with large gusts of wind. They're not intended to kill, just to make it quicker for him to reach his twin.

Frost is fighting hard. A wall of water is rolling over the beach, towards him and the demons. Is the water going to hurt him when it breaks over them?

Surely not. It's his element, after all.

I notice I'm gripping Crispin's hand. When did that happen?

Storm has almost reached his brother when the wave crashes over Frost and the demons surrounding him. For a moment, they're hidden from view. Storm skids to a halt, waiting for the water to disappear.

With bated breath, I wait. Every second feels like an hour. Then, the water wall that has stood upon the ground crashes down, releasing its victims. Demons collapse, drowned where they were standing. A few still move, but they don't pose a threat anymore. Frost stands in the middle of them, victorious.

And collapses.

Storm is by his brother's side in a flash. He lifts him up, obviously concerned. I wish I could understand what they're saying. He stretches an arm into the air, waving.

He needs Crispin's help.

"You ready?" I ask the healer.

"Yeah, let's do this. It's best if we circle the field as much as possible. It'll take longer, but if we get caught in the fighting it could mean we won't reach them at all."

I nod and release his hand. He pulls his sword from its sheath, and I do the same with my dagger. Into battle.

P rogress is slow. We're trying to stay out of sight, hiding behind low heather bushes and in an occasional ditch. It's a pity that this area has been landscaped for tourists who want to enjoy the view. There isn't much cover.

Once, we run into a demon struggler, but Crispin dispatches him with a single stroke. A drop of blood splatters on my face. But I don't have time to think about how disgusting it is, as Crispin takes my hand and drags me on.

Our original plan was that I'm to protect Crispin if we have to get to one of the Guardians. So far, it's been the other way around. I really need to start pulling my weight.

By the time we reach Frost and Storm, I'm covered in sweat and am having trouble breathing. I need to do more exercise. Maybe one of the Guardians can become my personal trainer once we're in the Realms. Or perhaps all of them. Of course they'd have to be topless to do that.

I'm grateful for my mind being silly as always. It distracts me from the dead demons littering the ground. One of them grips my ankle – okay, he's not quite dead yet. Instinctively, I bend down and stab him with my dagger. With a crunch, it sinks into his ribcage. There's almost no blood.

He lets loose of my foot and breathes his last breath.

My first kill.

I shudder.

"Wyn! Crispin! Over here!" Storm calls, his voice full of urgency.

Ignoring the dead demon at my feet, I run over to him. Frost is lying on the ground, his cheeks sporting a blue tinge. His eyes are closed and his breath is shallow. His armour lies discarded next to him, giving us a view of his pale upper body.

"What happened?" Crispin asks, his tone all business. This is Crispin the healer, not Crispin the friend.

"A demon stabbed him from behind, broke his concentration. The wound is shallow, but he lost control on the water and it almost drowned him, just like the demons."

"Turn him around," Crispin orders, and Storm gently rolls his brother on his stomach.

A large gash runs from Frost's left shoulder blade down to the bottom of his spine. It's bleeding heavily; his armour doesn't seem to have been strong enough to prevent the weapon reaching his skin. If this is what Storm describes as a 'shallow wound', I don't want to know what a deep wound would look like.

Crispin curses under his breath. "This will take a while. Wyn, look out for demons, you'll have to keep them away from us. Storm, the others will need your help. Go back and fight."

"He'll make it, right?" he grumbles.

"Yes, but none of us will make it if you don't kill those bastards," Crispin retorts, already waving his hand over Frost's unmoving body.

With a sigh, Storm takes his sword and turns away from us, running back to the battlefield. Two land spouts spring into life on either side of him. The fury of my Guardian is visible. I silently cheer him on. Demons hurt my Frost. They need to die.

I get up and take a protective stance in front of Crispin and his patient. Crispin is whispering under his breath, but it's too mumbled to understand.

I focus on our surroundings. A demon is approaching us, separating from the rest of the battle.

Brenda.

Shit.

I'm not sure I can deal with a higher demon yet.

"Crispin, there's a demon coming, but I'll get rid of her," I say with a confidence that is entirely made up.

I grasp my magic tightly, preparing to fight. This demon is going nowhere near my Guardians.

Now that she's coming closer, I get a better view of her hideousness. Her flesh looks like it's too large for her skin. Boils cover her arms and legs, but I'm not sure if they're from the battle or always like this. Sharp teeth are protruding from her puckered lips; they're totally out of proportion with the size of her mouth. A few hairs are stretched over her otherwise bald skull. She's the ugliest being I've ever seen.

And right now, she's smiling at me – if you can call it a smile. More a slight movement of her mouth.

"Daughter of Breia," she hisses. "It's time to die."

"Can't you come up with something more creative?" I yell back at her. "That's such an overused sentence."

She stares at me. Apparently, no one has called her out on her stereotypical phrases.

Then her smile grows broader and with a flick of her hand, the ground before me explodes. I'm thrown back; luckily not onto Crispin and Frost.

"Do you need help?" Crispin shouts. I want to say yes, but he's busy healing.

"I'll deal with her," I respond through clenched teeth. That bitch is going to die.

She wants to use magic against me? I'll show her my magic.

I don't even have to think about what to do. I simply reach into myself, take a bundle of magic and throw it in her direction. A huge fireball races towards her.

She shrieks, but manages to throw up a wall of earth in front of her just before the fire hits her. Damn it.

Let's try something else. I twist my hands and a whirlwind springs into being in front of me. I nudge it towards Brenda, and it shoots forward, crashing against her wall of earth. I twist my arm further and the wind turns into a small tornado, ripping through the earth, destroying her protective barrier.

I will the wind to move further, until it reaches the demon. She shrieks as it tears at her, ripping her few remaining hairs off her scalp. I laugh as I form another fire ball and throw it at her.

It mixes with the wind, turning the tornado into a burning torch. She screams as the flames touch her. Burn, demon bitch.

I channel more magic into the fire, willing it to burn even hotter. Her screams turn into wails, and I smile grimly as her skin begins to melt on her body. She threatened my Guardians. Now she's paying for it. They are mine.

"Wyn!" Crispin suddenly shouts, ripping me from my victorious rage. I turn around – and my heart drops. A demon is holding a knife to the healer's throat.

It's a small, unremarkable demon – he looks just like most of the other ones. But there's an intelligence burning behind his eyes that makes me categorise him as a higher demon immediately. This one is dangerous, probably more so than Brenda (who has now burned to a demon crisp behind me).

Crispin is looking more annoyed than scared. Well, guess I'm scared enough for both of us. That knife looks very sharp. And deadly.

"What do you want?" I snarl at the demon.

He laughs. "The same thing as every single one of us wants. You."

"Well, you're not getting me. Now release my friends."

I quiver with rage. I'm not going to let him get away with this.

He laughs even harder. "You're not in a position to make demands, abomination."

"What did you just call me?"

He grins widely, saliva forming a spider's web around his crooked teeth.

"You're a halfling. A bastard. An abomination born of incest. You should have been killed when you were born. Now my Mistress is making things right. And I will be the one to do it. She'll reward m—"

He drops to the ground, taking the knife with him. A tiny drop of blood runs down Crispin's throat. He wipes it off with his hand. Strange how he is wounded, but the demon lies dead on the ground, no sign of injury. He could be sleeping. Nobody will know how I stopped his heart with just a single tendril of magic. Except for Crispin, of course.

"Couldn't you have done that a little earlier?" he huffs.

"Sorry, couldn't decide how to do it. It's strange, his heart looked just like a human one."

He smiles sadly. "You're a good student. But I wish you wouldn't have had to do that."

Actually, I'm glad. Stopping that demon's heart was the best thing I've ever done. I'm glowing inside. I want to jump and tell the world. Then I want to burn it.

"I'm going to kill some demons," I announce and leave the two Guardians, ignoring Crispin's protest. I stride onto the battlefield, looking for demons to kill. My magic is sharpening her claws inside me, purring at the thought of demon blood pouring onto the ground.

No one is going to stop us.

I'm a demi-goddess. These demons are no match for me.

I'm feeling a little hot, so I conjure fire balls and let them rain down on the battle field. Demons shriek all around me, running away from their burning comrades. I laugh as heather brush catches fire on the ground. Thick smoke is beginning to rise, making it hard to see. But I don't care. I throw more fire all around me, not caring whether it actually hits someone.

I'm drunk on magic, and it's the best feeling ever.

A demon runs at me from behind, but I know he's coming and send a fiery lance towards him. It rips a hole into his abdomen, and for a moment, I can look through him, until he collapses to the ground.

A few more demons are running towards me. I smile and form a few fire whips and wrap them around their necks, cleanly slicing through them. Four demons less.

Maybe I should see if Arc needs help. He doesn't have destructive powers like me and the other Guardians.

I skip across the battlefield like a child, ignoring the dead demons all around me. I haven't had this fun in a long time.

I feel for my bond to Arc, and turn into his direction. He's not far. A few more demons get in my way, but I kill them with more fire lances. This is so easy. At least Brenda was a challenge, but these demons are nothing but critters that I can crush with a single thought.

I wave when I see Arc, shooting fire into the air. Oops, that wasn't the plan. He looks at me strangely, and I turn to see if there are demons behind me, but I've burnt them all.

There's a demon next to Arc, though. She's not going to hurt my Arc.

I ready a fire ball.

"Arc, get out of the way!" I shout, but strangely enough, he shifts until he's standing in front of the demon.

As if he's protecting her.

What the fuck?

She's a demon, she needs to die. All demons need to die. That's the way it is.

"She's going to kill you, get away from her!" I warn him, but he's just shaking his head.

"Snap out of it, lass! It's Chesca! Ye ken Chesca, she's not like the others!"

Somehow that rings a bell, but the fire in me extinguishes that thought.

"One last time, get away from her!" I shout.

"Or what? You're going to burn me?"

No, I'm not. Right? But there's a demon, and she needs to be killed. My magic is growling. She wants blood. Demon blood.

Not letting go of my fire ball, I conjure a wind lasso with my other hand, just like the ones I used this morning to get Storm off me. I wrap it around Arc's waist and pull, ripping him away from the demon. He flies through the air and I'm sure the landing isn't too comfortable for him, but he's safe now.

Finally, I can throw that fire ball at the demon. I grin and send it towards her, but – she's no longer there. She's extended her wings and is flying a few metres above the battlefield.

We can't have that. I shoot some more fire at her, but she's too quick and easily evades them. Time to change tactics. I form a wind lasso and swing it around her, aiming to pull her down to the ground so I can burn her and –

I'm wrestled to the ground. I prepare to shoot fire at them, but then I see Arc's green eyes and retract my magic. My

Guardian. Why is he looking at me so strangely? Isn't he proud of me?

"Wyn, ye need ta stop," he whispers.

"But they need to die," I protest, but he shushes me.

"This isn't you. The magic is controlling ya. I can help ya, but ye need ta lower yer barriers for a moment, lass."

His voice is calm and soothing, and I want to do what he tells me to. But the magic isn't letting me. She's clawing at me, urging me to get rid of him so she can kill more demons.

I take a deep breath. He's asked for it. This isn't on me.

I reach for my magic – and stop as I feel something strange happening. It takes me a moment to realise that it's a weird kind of scratching at the shield around my mind. I take a look at my island. It's still surrounded by my glass sphere, just as I left it. But something is knocking against it from the outside. Someone.

My ginger Guardian.

I run to him, everything else forgotten. He puts his hands against the glass, and I do the same on my side of the barrier. Suddenly, the glass disappears and his hands grasp mine. A second later, he stands next to me.

"Quickly, mend the shield."

Confused, I do as he says and fix the hole.

"How did you do that?" I ask him once the sphere is whole again.

He smirks. "Trade secret. Now, what do ye think ye were doing out there? Are ye mad?"

"I was killing dem—" I gasp.

What did I do?

What the hell happened?

What the fuck is wrong with me?

I press my hands against my mouth, suddenly feeling queasy. All that blood I spilled. All those demons I killed. The wounds I inflicted. The joy I felt while doing it.

I retch, bending over. But nothing comes out. Guess puking doesn't work in the mind.

"It's okay, lass," Arc says soothingly, rubbing my back. I stand up and lean into his hug. His strong arms press me against his body and I feel guilty for enjoying it.

I should be punished. I shouldn't be comforted. I don't deserve it.

We stand on the beach, joined in our hug, for a long time.

Finally, I ask the question that has been drumming in my mind the whole time. "Why did I do this? How could I?"

"Yer magic took control of ya. Yer not experienced enough to use so much magic at once. Remember the earthquake?"

I nod. How could I not? I levelled a street.

"Some elements have a stronger effect on ya. Looks like fire and earth are yer strongest elements, but they're also harder ta control. Have ye felt the same with any others?"

I think back to the start of the battle.

I used wind to capture Brenda, but it didn't affect me in the way fire had done. I hadn't used water, so no idea about that one. And when I stopped the demon's heart, it had been quick and I didn't feel happy about it. Not like with fire. I had revelled in the flames devouring demon flesh.

I shudder. "No, but I haven't used water yet. Wind seems to be safe."

"Then stick to wind as much as ye can. But first, we need ta get ye back ta Crispin." He looks down at me, his eyes softening. "Do ye need more time, wee one? This is all in yer mind, there's almost nae time passing in the real world."

"Yes. I'd rather not face Chesca just now."

He chuckles. "She'll be mad, no doubt aboot that. But it was a nice move, the way ye pulled me away from her. Yer skills are improving."

"Let's not talk about the battle, please," I whisper. "I don't want to think about it just yet. For now, I just want to enjoy how you –" I better shut up now.

"How I what, lass?"

In response, I rub my cheek against his chest. He's not wearing armour here, just a tight t-shirt that is highlighting his muscles. He runs a hand through my hair. He gently moves my neck until I'm looking up at him and his beautiful green eyes.

"How I what?" he repeats.

I blush. "Feel. You feel good. Okay? You feel amazing, smell amazing, look amazing. And I really shouldn't be saying all this, but apparently, I don't have much of a filter in here."

He laughs, his chest vibrating against my cheek. I love it when he does that. "I'll show ye how amazing I feel." And presses his lips against mine. I hungrily open my mouth, inviting him in. He kisses me with a passion that surpasses any other kiss. Ever.

He runs his hands over my back, drawing circles on my skin. I can feel my tense muscles relax. I moan as he leaves my lips to take a breath.

"So impatient," he chuckles. "We shouldnae do this, Princess. But I cannae stop." With that, he plunges his tongue back into my mouth, and I meet him with my own. I slide my hands under his shirt and explore his soft skin. It's amazing how silky it feels, even though the muscles underneath are rock hard. Just like another part of him that is pressing against my stomach.

He said that time wouldn't pass in the real world while we're in here, right? So there's no reason not to move my hands down towards his tight arse and squeeze a little, causing him to gasp while still having his lips pressed against mine. I smile and nibble on his bottom lip. In response, he squeezes my bum, pressing me even closer against his body.

I'm so aroused; I need more. Without warning, I step back and pull my shirt over my head. He chortles. "Keen, are ye?"

"I need to feel more of you," I say simply, and look into his eyes. They're like molten emeralds, full of emotion and softness. He smiles and takes off his own shirt, exposing his sculptured body. Seriously, are Guardians made this way or do they have to go to a gym? If I was a Goddess, I guess I'd create them hot like this – I mean, having some eye candy walking around your palace can't hurt.

"Take off the rest," Arc growls as he steps out of his own jeans. Suddenly I'm a little shy. And worried that this is totally inappropriate. Who ever thought of having sex during a battle? Even if it's only in my mind. Especially...

"Arc, I really want you. I really, really do. But shouldn't our first time be in the real world?"

He stares at me for a moment. Me, in my bra, my nipples poking through the lacy fabric. My flushed cheeks. My hair, probably standing in all directions from when his hands ran through it. Basically, I must look like a girl ready for a Guardian to take her here and now.

"Aye, ye're right," he finally says. He pulls me closer again until skin touches skin. "But that doesn't mean we have ta stop completely."

He kisses me again, softer this time, like he's saying goodbye. I'm shouting at myself. Why did I have to be so... sensible? Couldn't I just have gone with the flow? Damn it, Wyn. You just missed out on sleeping with a yummy Guardian. Bet no other girl would ever voluntarily miss out on that.

I slowly draw my fingers over his back, my nails leaving gentle scratches. With one hand on the back of my hand, he pulls me closer into our kiss. With the other, he presses my belly against his pelvis, where something hard will end up disappointed today.

Maybe later. After the battle.

With a final flick of his tongue against my lips, he ends the kiss.

Chapter Sixteen

"You're late to the party," Chesca says, sitting on the body of the fiend I saw earlier. His wings have been torn off and his face is... well, not very face-like anymore.

Remind me not to cross Chesca. And please make her forget that I attacked her earlier. That wasn't me. That was my magic.

Only now do I take in my surroundings. The ground is littered with dead demons. Burnt demons, mostly. Further away, demons are still fighting, but we are standing in a bloody clearing. An acrid smell hangs in the air. Something like the smell of burned hair mixed with that of steak and dog poo. I try to breathe through my mouth, but the smell still reaches my nose.

"Did I do all that?" I ask quietly, shocked by the sheer devastation.

"Yeah, sure you did," Chesca said cheerily, still sitting on the fiend corpse. "It was so magnificent that I'd almost forgive you for attacking me." She stands up in a flash and pokes me in the chest with a clawed finger. "But only almost. I'm going to come up with a nice punishment for you, little princess. Maybe I'll steal one of your Guardians."

Maybe I deserve that. But then my magic rears up in me. Mine.

I snarl. "If you want my Guardians, you'll have to go over my dead body." So cliché, but it's true. I won't let anyone else have them.

And I'm beginning to think that it's not just because of the bond and the ritual. No, it's something much deeper than that. They are special. And mine. End of. If they want it or not.

Suddenly, Chesca shrieks and points to something behind us, I turn and - a small fireball is exploding in the sky. Aodh is in trouble.

We run over the battlefield to where the flare came from. Each of us has a signal for when we need help. A fiery ball in the sky is Aodh's. Chesca extends her wings and jumps into the air, quickly leaving us behind as we try to run without stumbling over corpses. A large group of demons is fighting not far from the visitor centre. That means Aodh hasn't moved far since the battle started. He's strong, but there are a lot of demons there - at least twenty, in all shapes and sizes. At least I can't see one of the higher demons we identified earlier. Three of them are dead, but I don't know if the others have been killed yet. Let's hope so.

When we reach the first demon, I throw him to the ground with a sharp burst of air, ready for Arc to stab him in the chest. We dispatch three more in that way. Quite the team, I think morbidly.

Chesca's wail breaks through the sound of fighting. A moment later, a gap opens in the demon ranks and I can finally see - and regret it immediately. Aodh is lying on the ground, surrounded by dead demons. I can't see his face, and he's too far away to tell whether he's still breathing. Chesca and Storm are standing above him, fighting the demon onslaught. Chesca is using her wings to slash through the demons in front of her; apparently, those wings are a lot sturdier (and deadlier) than they look. Storm is fighting with his sword, not his magic, hacking at demons, crippling or killing them with each stroke. He's looking magnificent. Every move is practiced. It's a beautiful slaughter.

"Watch out!" Arc yells next to me and I turn around to see a group of demons running towards us. Great. Just what we needed.

I decide not to use my fire magic again. Yes, it's effective, but I don't want to risk losing control again. Instead, I reach into the earth, gripping it tightly, then throw it against the oncoming demons. A wall of mud rises from the ground and slams into them, burying them. I immediately let go of my connection to the earth. Not planning to cause another earthquake.

"Well done!" Arc shouts while freezing three demons with his mind, only to stab them one after the other. "That was good control."

Is he really telling me that I'm getting better at killing demons? No thanks, not a skill I want to excel at.

"We could use some help here!" Storm yells and I turn, looking for the best way to kill the demons beleaguering him and the others. More have joined the fray. There seems to be no end to the demons ready to kill us all.

This needs to be precise; the demons are too close to my friends for large scale attacks. There is a way, but do I dare to do it? Chesca shrieks in fury as a sword cuts into her wing. Black blood drips on the ground. I need to act now.

"Arc, keep them away from me for a moment," I order, and close my eyes, trusting in my Guardian's ability to keep me safe.

I feel for their hearts - it's like I've always done this. It's too easy. I can snuff them all out in a second. Why have I wasted to much energy on fighting with the elements? I could have just killed all the demons in one go.

I can hear shouts from far away. No time to waste. I focus and with a single thought, I extinguish thirty demon hearts at once.

And then I know why nobody does this.

Black energy rams into me from thirty demon hearts.

My magic screams, and I scream, and then everything goes as black as the foreign power raging within me.

I wake to the sound of sobs. Which makes me want to fall unconscious again immediately. They are heart-wrenching, terrifying sobs. And even though my head is pounding and my body feels like it's been run over by a half-ton demon, I know that it's Chesca who's crying.

And I can guess why.

Aodh.

I remember the fire Guardian, lying on the ground, his face turned away from me, surrounded by battling demons and their fallen brothers.

Aodh, laughing at the cottage when I tried not to cringe after tasting Chesca's scones.

Aodh, looking concerned when I arrived with a badly burnt Frost.

Aodh, a Guardian who actually managed to tame a demon.

I can feel a tear running down my face.

"Wyn, are you awake?" Crispin asks.

I want to open my mouth to reply - but I can't move my lips. In panic, I try to wiggle my toes, lift my arms, but nothing is happening. I groan, but no sound escapes my throat.

I am locked in.

"Princess, squeeze my hand," my healer Guardian asks, his voice filled with concern.

I try as hard as I can, but my fingers don't even twitch.

By now, I'm fully awake. My mind, that is. I reach into myself to look for my magic. Maybe I can use it to send them a message.

I reach my heart cave, and stare at it in shock. The entrance has collapsed; large boulders stop me from entering. My magic, where is she? Trapped inside, like I am trapped within my body? I try to shift one of the smaller boulders, but it's too heavy. Magic would come in handy just now.

I kick the stone in front of me, yelling at the pain in my toes. I know this isn't real, but it certainly feels like it is. It's more real than the world outside my body, the world I can't interact with.

What the hell did I do to end up in this situation?

Why did I have to try and kill so many demons at once?

Why didn't anyone warn me?

I kick the stone again, and this time I'm revelling in the pain.

It's my penance for the Guardian I killed and the demons I destroyed. My rightful punishment. Me, locked in my body, having to deal with it all instead of laughing it off like I usually do.

I want to cry, but instead, I scream. All I get back in return is my echo.

I curl up at the cave's entrance, hugging my knees to my chest. Aodh's face is flashing in front of my eyes. I only knew him for a day, but I grieve for him nonetheless.

He died for me.

I didn't protest when he offered to fight.

I never even thought about it.

No, I was so obsessed with my own fears and worries that I never considered that it might be wrong to ask so much of him and Chesca.

Now he's dead.

Light blinds me. Someone is opening my eyes. I'm looking into blue sky. I try to look to the side, but nothing happens. Great, I can't even move my eyes. A blurry face appears, hiding the sky. Crispin.

He's looking straight into my eyes. I try to blink, move, do something to show him that I'm alive in here. But after a moment, he lets my eyelid fall shut and darkness surrounds me once more.

Actually, that's not quite true. I see orange, lots of reddish orange. My eyes are seeing, even though they're not open.

I think I'd prefer black, I've always hated the colour orange.

"Why aren't you fixing her?!" Storm's loud voice breaks the silence. There is panic in it, and desperation. If Crispin isn't healing me, something must be seriously wrong.

"Her body is fine, I've healed the few scratches she had from the fight. But her magic... something is wrong with it. I've never seen anything like it, though. It's as if it's shielded, but I can't see through the shield. It's different from a mental shield, it's slippery and just... wrong."

"Let me try." Arc's voice is coming closer and the sound of someone kneeling beside me reaches my ears.

Silence falls. I wait for something to happen. Maybe Arc will appear to me like he did when he was outside my island sphere. Maybe he'll manage to talk to me.

The bond! Maybe I can communicate through my bond! I've got hope for a second - then I remember that I use my magic to tug on my connection to the guys. No magic, no bond.

"I cannae reach her," Arc sighs, and I can feel a hand gently running over my cheek.

"Then try again!" Storm shouts. Inside, I cry for him. He's so angry, so desperate.

"He's doing what he can," Frost's gentle voice comes from far away. That's so like him, calming his brother, but not getting the chance to do something himself.

"Watch out!" Crispin suddenly yells, and the ground rumbles below me. Something explodes close by and a blast of hot air hits me. A body falls on top of me - or maybe throws itself.

Damn it, why do I still feel pain. Could I just be numb, please? Preferably in my mind as well.

"It's Lewan, I thought ya killed him, Storm!" Arc shouts.

"I thought you killed him!"

Someone huffs in frustration above me. Frost. Oh, it's him who's lying on top of my body. "Would either of you please kill Lewan? It's getting a little hot here!"

He's right, it feels like something is burning around us. The air is beginning to hurt when I breathe in, it's that hot.

"On it," Storm growls.

More explosions. Then the sound of wind, lots of wind. Shrieks in the distance.

Then silence. The heat ebbs away.

Apparently, whoever attacked us is no longer able to do so. Hopefully he's lying on the battlefield - in pieces.

Frost gets up, leaving me alone on the ground.

"Looks like he was just a straggler," Storm grumbles.

"Some fled when Wyn killed the demons around us, so they might come back. We need to get through that Gate as soon as possible."

Chapter Seventeen

My body is lifted by one of the guys. I'm pressed against a hard leather breast plate. They are still wearing their armour. It's hard to tell who is carrying me – they're all broad and muscly and wear armour. And they all smell of blood right now.

But then, does it matter? They're all my Guardians.

I am pressed close against the guy's chest. There's an arm under my knees and another wrapped around my back. It's not uncomfortable, but the swaying without being able to see what's happening, is making me queasy. What happens if I need to puke? Will I choke on my own vomit, unable to open my mouth? I decide not to find out.

There's an eerie silence around us. The guys aren't talking, and I can't. Apparently, there are no demons left at Calanais. The battle was so chaotic, I totally lost track of how many we killed. How many I killed.

It was necessary, but I know that I will never forget the smell of blood and burned demon that is now wafting over the battlefield. It's a miracle, really, that we all managed to get out relatively unscathed. With 'we', I mean the Guardians and me. I don't want to think of Aodh and Chesca.

Where is Chesca, by the way? She must have left while I was unconscious. I don't think she could stay quiet for this long.

We finally stop and the queasiness slowly disappears from my stomach.

"Are you ready?" Storm asks quietly.

"Aye."

"Yes."

"Yes." The last one to speak is Frost, close to my ear. He's the one carrying me. "But do you think this is safe? She won't be able to think of our destination when we step through the Stones."

"We should probably all hold onto her," Crispin suggests. "Arc, have you contacted the healers on the other side?"

"Aye, they're ready. Perhaps they ken what's wrong with the lass."

"Stand close together and hold her tightly," Storm commands.

Three pairs of hands are gripping my body in various places. There's a grumble inside of me. I dive deep until I'm in front of my heart cave. One of the large boulders blocking the entrance has split in half! There are still many others obstructing my connection to my magic, but something changed. It must have been their touch; this can't have been a coincidence.

"3...2...1...go!"

We step through the Gate.

I'm flying on a rainbow. A fucking rainbow.

Everything is bright and colourful and magical. Magic! I can feel my magic! She's not inside of me though, no, she's floating by my side, purring as the wind tousles her fur. She's stretching her limbs; finally out of the cave I have kept her in for so long. She grins at me, and I smile back. We're friends, taking a ride on a rainbow that looks like a unicorn belched while flying loops through the air. It's not a rainbow that starts on the ground and then forms a half circle. No, this rainbow is like a rollercoaster, stretching infinitely into the distance, shaped in curves and loops and – is that a heart shape up there?

This must be a dream. A very lucid one, though. It feels so real. Have I taken drugs?

"Wyn!" someone shouts from behind me, casting a chiming echo through this rainbow world. It's Storm, riding the rainbow like a surfer rides a wave. I laugh and try to swim against the flow to reach him, but it doesn't work. Luckily, he's an expert rainbow-rider and reaches me in no time.

"Wyn," he rasps, and then I'm in his arms, squeezed against his chest. My magic chuckles and moves further ahead, giving us some space. I never thought she'd be this considerate.

Storm lifts my head with a finger gently held beneath my chin. His eyes are soft, and he's actually smiling at me. Storm, smiling! This must be a dream.

He comes closer until our lips almost touch. "I thought I'd lost you," he whispers, his breath hot against my skin.

I'm trying to come up with a reply, but my mind is blank. So I do the next best thing: I get up on my toes and kiss him. He groans and nudges my lips open with his tongue. He's starting out gently, but after a few soft kisses, they turn wilder. While claiming my mouth, he slides his hands under my shirt.

I moan as he breaks our kiss.

"Don't worry, Princess, I'm not finished yet," Storm growls, and rips my shirt in two. How the hell did he do that? But I couldn't care less when he unhooks my bra and takes it off, together with the remains of my shirt. He goes on his knees in front of me and looks up with a strange look in his eyes. Desire? Devotion? Admiration? Hard to tell. He kisses the soft skin between my breasts and I moan again. While he's leaving a trail of kisses down over my belly, he grabs my bum with his hands. I push my pelvis forwards, an open invitation. He chuckles.

"Patience."

"Since when are you promoting patience?"

In response, he unzips my jeans and slides them down, encouraging me to step out of them. All I'm wearing now are my panties (and my shoes, but that doesn't count). I wish I had put on some nicer ones, but when I prepared for battle this morning, wearing pretty underwear wasn't high up on my agenda.

Kneading my arse, he continues to leave gentle kisses just below my belly button. It tickles and I'm getting frustrated with him. It's not enough.

Suddenly, there are hands on my breasts. Before I can turn around, a teasing voice whispers in my ear, "Guess I shouldn't have worried about you. Seems like my brother is looking after you already. You do know we've still got a way to go to reach the other side of the Gate?"

Frost.

Storm shoots an annoyed glance at his brother. "We don't know if she will be okay once we reach the other side. Let's stay in here a while longer."

"I'm okay with that," Frost chuckles, and begins to gently massage my breasts. I lean into him, and he bends his head, nibbling on the nape of my neck. How does that feel so good?

Storm has finally decided to do the right thing, and is slowly pulling down my panties. When his mouth touches the skin just above that spot, I see rainbows. Okay, maybe I've been seeing them all the time because we're standing on one. But you get what I mean.

I close my eyes as my body fills with pleasure. I'm in the arms of two Guardians. Unbelievable. Frost is twisting my nipples between his fingers while grazing my neck with his teeth. For some reason, I want him to bite me. Not something I've ever wanted before. What are those guys doing to me?

Something presses against my core. Instinctively, I spread my legs a little. I cry out when Storm slides his finger inside me while suckling on my bud at the same time. Damn that Guardian!

If Frost wasn't holding me, I'd be writhing on the floor by now.

"Open wide for my brother," Frost whispers, sliding his hands down my belly until he reaches my pelvis. Storm adds another finger and as instructed, I spread my legs further, giving him better access. His tongue is driving me crazy, flicking and suckling and swirling.

A roaring laughter interrupts us. I open my eyes and see Arc and Crispin running towards us. Is it really bad that I want them all? "Don't stop," I command, and use my hands to press Storm's head between my legs again.

"Can we join?" Arc asks as they reach us.

Crispin shakes his head in frustration. "Has anyone actually thought to ask why she is standing here, conscious? Or are you all thinking with your dicks today?"

Storm refuses to answer, instead focussing on bringing me pleasure. Works for me.

Frost clears his throat. "Well, she's obviously okay, and I thought Storm had..."

"Typical! Wyn, I should examine you," Crispin says matter-of-factly.

Storm growls. "Piss off or join us."

Arc gives me a mock bow. "Princess, with yer permission?"

I'm too busy trying not to completely let go of all inhibition, so I just nod. The more, the merrier. A small voice in my head is telling me that this isn't me, that I'm too prude for this, but I don't care. I've got three hot Guardians around me, all intending to make me feel good.

Arc is by my side in seconds, grasping my hair with one hand and pulling me towards him. He claims my mouth at the same moment as Storm adds a third finger. Gods, this is amazing. Frost is hard against my back and with every thrust of his brother's fingers, I rub further against him.

Around us, the rainbow is sparkling. But maybe that is just my mind making up weird things in the heat of the moment.

This. Feels. So. Good.

Storm suddenly stops the amazing tongue work he's been doing. Damn that Guardian. I was so close. "Crispin, would you like to..." He falters as he looks behind him where our healer stood a moment ago.

Crispin is gone.

"Dinnae worry, Princess," Arc mumbles while stopping his wild kiss for a moment. "He's not been with a lass in a long time. We dinnae ken what's wrong with him. Just forget aboot it, it's got nothing ta do with ya."

I can't reply because his lips cover mine once more, and his tongue meets mine in an ecstatic dance. Storm slides his fingers out of me and suddenly I feel very empty. I moan against Arc's mouth. Then I hear the sound of a zip though, and I know it's not over yet.

"Lie her down," Storm says breathlessly. Gently, Frost lowers me to the ground. My breasts are swollen from the attention he's been giving them. Once I'm flat on the ground, he bends over them, taking one of my nipples into his mouth. Arc suckles on the other, while Storm spreads my legs.

Sweet Gods, am I really surrounded by three Guardians? Three hot, sexy, talented guys who make me feel better than any man has ever before.

Storm slides a finger into me again and I arch my pelvis in response, inviting him in. Then I remember that I want more.

"Storm, please," I moan, but Arc slides a finger into my mouth and silences me. I suck on it, and for some reason that feels amazing.

"Princess, you ready?" Storm asks and I lift my head to look at him. He's naked, and beautiful, and rock hard. Are all Guardians that... big? I guess I'll have to do research...

"Are you sure you want this?" Storm asks again and I nibble on Arc's finger until he pulls it out of my mouth.

"Yes, I want you," I whisper, not taking my eyes off him.

"And you don't want me?" Frost asks. I'm not sure if he's joking or if he's offended.

"I want you all."

Frost smiles and bends down, kissing me hard. I notice that my hands are lying uselessly on the ground, so I reach up and pull Arc towards me. I need all my Guardians close. That's the moment Storm enters me. He's not gentle, or slow. He pushes in and I groan in pleasure as he fills me. We're one, and many. He moves in me, and at the same time, Frost is kissing me and Arc is massaging my breasts while I touch the bulge between his legs.

We are one.

Storm is sliding in and out of me, harder and harder. I'm starting to lose control; my breath has grown erratic and my hands are balled into fists, waiting for release. Frost pulls back for a moment, and I inhale deeply. There are sparks all around us, flittering through the air like fireflies. They're tiny, but shimmering in a thousand colours. "Can you see them?" I whisper, unsure if this is just my eyes playing tricks on me.

Storm stops for a moment and I regret having asked the question. Couldn't my curiosity have waited for just a few more minutes. Well, hours. Hopefully.

Then he slams back into me and I squeal. "Yes." He slides out. "I can see them." And pushes in again, setting a new, fast rhythm. I won't last much longer.

The little sparks are forming shapes in the air, pulsing spirals, strange glittery clouds,

Something is happening. But I couldn't care less just now. My mind is blank, all that counts is the heat flooding my body, the electricity flowing through my nerves. I'm close. Someone starts rubbing my clit, but I've got my eyes closed, and it doesn't matter. It feels good. More than good. I'm floating on a cloud of bliss.

"Wyn," Storm groans, and I moan with him as he jerks and presses deep inside me, coming at the same time as my inner walls contract, hugging him tightly. I ride the climax, my body one big haven of pleasure. There are hands on me, gently stroking my skin, but I'm too exhausted to reciprocate. My Guardians, surrounding me. Storm, still inside me.

The bond is pulsating within me, and from afar I can hear my magic purr. Finally, they are satisfied.

I slowly drift back into reality. Well, whatever crazy rainbow reality we're in, anyway. I open my eyes - and blink a few times. I'm covered in glitter. The little sparkly particles that have been floating around the air have landed on my skin - they're everywhere! I look like a... well, like I stood at the wrong end of a flatulent unicorn. I lift an arm in wonder, mesmerised by the glitter reflecting the rainbow light around me.

"What the fuck is happening?" I finally ask. Judging from their confused looks, my Guardians don't know either. Storm slides out of me, leaving me with an empty feeling. I'm exhausted, but I want more. I want Frost and Arc. And Storm, again. Together, on a rainbow, covered in glitter.

I giggle, which quickly turns into a giddy laugh.

"You've broken her," Frost accuses his brother. "Now she's behaving like a... girl." He shudders as I break out in more giggles.

"I've never seen anything like this," Storm finally says.

"It looks like magic. Magic that isn't bound," Arc ponders, his forehead scrunched. He probably doesn't realise that he's still having a hand on my boobs. I won't tell him. The glitter doesn't seem to hurt him, so why break the delicious touch?

"But magic is always bound. It can't exist without an anchor," Storm argues. "Otherwise it would float around and do Gods-know-what. Explosions. Mutations. That kind of stuff."

I frown, the giggles suddenly gone. "Wait, so this stuff doesn't usually float around in this rainbow?"

"Rainbow?!" Storm looks at me incredulously.

"You've not noticed that we're standing on a rainbow?"

"We're on a cloud—"

"No, we're on a wave," Frost interrupts his brother.

"Lightning," Arc mutters.

"So, we're each seeing something different. How can you not know that? You've travelled through this Gate before, right?"

They look at each other.

"Aye, but usually we step in on one side and out of the other one. There's nothing in between. Nae rainbows, nae magic. Nae... sex."

I cover my face in my hands. "Is this even real?"

Frost pinches me on my hip and I yelp. He grins innocently. "Looks like it's real."

Bastard.

"Now can we get back ta the fun stuff?" Arc asks and takes his hand off my boob - and everything spins as I'm pulled away from them, along the rainbow, flying through the air, faster and faster, a cloud of glitter flying behind me. I scream. Then suddenly, there's a loop, a damn big rollercoaster loop. I flail, trying to get rid of the pull that is making me race along the rainbow, up the loop and - no, please don't let me fall - down again. I try to keep the contents of my stomach down as I spin around my own axis, unsure of what's up and what's down.

The rainbow stops and there's nothing beyond.

An invisible force grabs me and throws me and -

- I land on soft snow. There's no harsh impact, no pain. The freezing cold gnawing on my skin is letting me know that I'm still naked. Damn those boys. And where are they anyway? I look around. Behind me is a beautiful iron-wrought gate, covered in frost ferns and tiny icicles. Beyond that... a rainbow.

So it was real. The pulsing between my legs confirms that. I look down at myself. The glitter has gone, thank the Gods.

The Gate flickers and a crackling noise fills the air. From beyond the rainbow, four large shapes materialise. They grow bigger, coming closer, until my Guardians step out of the Gate. So graceful. None of them fall down like I did. Typical.

And Crispin has joined them somehow. Weird.

I sit up, but something pulls me back. I must be stuck to something on the ground. I turn to see what it is, but a collective gasp from my Guardians makes me look back at them. They're staring at me, wide-eyed.

"Look at her! She's got... wings!"

Chapter Eighteen

ings.

The word echoes in my mind.

Wings.

How the hell can I have wings? I'm not an angel (definitely not, just ask my adoptive parents). Not a demon, either (I'm not that bad). So why do I have wings?

They're not like the demon wings I saw during the battle, all leathery and thick. Nor are they like bird wings. No, they're like... shimmering dust, gathered together until it forms a half-translucent shape. Delicate, like butterfly wings, but even thinner. They're all the colours of the rainbow, but purple seems to be slightly dominant. I bend my arms so I can touch where they grow from my back. Nothing. It feels like always, just smooth skin, no weird bone spurts, no feathers, nothing. I can touch the wings, though. And put my hands through them. They're like gelatine - there is a resistance, but with enough pressure, you can push your way through it.

Somehow, I make them flutter. No idea how, but some unknown muscles do it for me. Or magic. Probably the latter.

"She's got wings," Frost huffs, still as wide-eyed as the other Guardians.

"We can see that," Arc adds, looking at me like he's never seen me before. I must make an interesting sight. Naked, with rainbow wings, in the snow.

Did I mention my life doesn't make much sense?

"You must be cold, Princess," Crispin says and comes to me, offering me his jacket. Finally, one of them has some practical thoughts. I shiver and wrap myself in the leather jacket. It smells like Crispin; a slight scent of pine and aniseed. My lower body is exposed and -

Wait, I just wrapped clothing around my wings. Shouldn't that hurt? Or at least be uncomfortable? I look over my shoulder. They are gone.

"They were there a moment ago, right?" I ask, my voice faltering.

With a sigh, Storm pulls his shirt over his head. And shows me his wings.

Wow.

They're similar to mine, but much larger, and not translucent at all. The tips are above his head, and the lowest point is just above his knees. They're a dark blue, almost black, and shimmer in the bright light of the snowy landscape.

"You have wings. But you didn't have wings before," I stutter, totally in shock.

"Guys, show her," Storm commands, and the other three Guardians take off their shirts (and in Arc's case, part of the armour he's still wearing). Three pairs of wings unfold and take my breath away. Frost's are a turquoise blue, with darker sapphire hues that weave across them like waves on an ocean. Arc's are a dark copper, but the tips shine ruby red. And Crispin's are... well, golden, matching his blonde hair.

I must be staring at them for minutes, trying to get my head around the fact that they have wings.

Then I snap. This is too much. "Why the hell didn't you tell me? Why do I have wings? Why do I know how to move them? And why...?"

Crispin shushes me by taking me into his arms.

"It's okay, darling, everything will make sense soon," he whispers. But I want it to make sense now! I'm close to stomping on the ground, but that would be childish. It's just too much for my brain to take. First, locked into my body, then having sex on a rainbow, and now we all have wings. Somehow that sounds like a bad trip. Maybe I'm still at home, having taken drugs with friends. But I don't do drugs, and I don't have many friends either. So maybe not.

"Damn it, why do you need to have wings? Weren't you perfect enough already?" I mutter against Crispin's naked chest. He chuckles. "You've got them too. No idea why, but you have them. And they are beautiful."

With a sigh, I step back, leaving the comfort of his arms. "How can they just disappear like that?"

"Magic," Arc grins. "Everything here is magic. Ya'll see, and ya'll love it."

Yeah, not too sure about that. It's all a bit of a shock.

I look around us. There's nothing but snow and more snow. The Gate is the only distinctive feature in this icy landscape.

"Weren't there supposed to be other Guardians awaiting us?" I ask.

"Yes, there were," Storm answers grimly, putting his shirt back on. "Arc, find out where they are."

Arc nods and closes his eyes, furrowing his brow. A moment later, he opens them again, sighing deeply. "They were called away by the Queen. An emergency, Thomas says."

Storm frowns. "It must have been important. She wouldn't leave her daughter in danger just for nothing."

I chuckle mirthlessly. "She's left me alone all my life. Why would that change now."

Arc puts an arm around my shoulders. "She'll explain soon, lass. It was fer a good reason."

"Yeah, I'm sure it was," I huff. I'll decide that when I hear the explanation. Somehow, I can't think of anything that would justify leaving your child in another world, only seeing her a few times in twenty-two years. What mother would do that?

"Look!", Frost shouts suddenly, pointing towards the sky. I look up - and gasp as a group of Guardians are flying towards us. They look like gigantic birds at first, but as they're coming closer, I am beginning to see their features. Three men, one woman. The first female Guardian I'm seeing. If she is a Guardian. But then, Crispin had a sister, so female Guardians must exist. Her white-blonde hair is forming a long trail behind her - think comet, but humanoid. Her hair must reach to her feet, at least. Her skin is dark mocha beneath a black jumpsuit; a stark contrast to the light hair and silver wings. Even from a distance, she's stunning. The three men around her all look the same. Dark blue clothes, dark blue wings, dark blue hair. Their ivory skin is the only thing on them that isn't dark blue. Whoever created them must have been obsessed with that colour.

They land a hundred yards or so away from us, gracefully gliding onto the ground before folding their wings. The woman steps forward, flanked by the three men. They must be triplets; it's impossible to tell them apart.

When she reaches us, she bows deeply, and the males follow her lead a moment later.

"Princess, welcome to the Winter Realm. I am Ada, and these are Fox, Lynx and Phoenix. We have been sent by her majesty to escort you to the palace."

I'm not quite sure how to respond, so I simply incline my head and say, "Thank you."

Until now, she has ignored my Guardians, who have taken up position behind me. Two on each side. Protective, but not overpowering. My heart warms at the thought of having all four of them so close to me. I will need them in this strange world.

Pointedly avoiding looking at my half-nakedness, Ada hands me a blue uniform; the same that her Guardians are wearing. I gratefully put it on (while I make everyone turn around), revelling in the warmth.

"We have brought a PT to transport you to the capital," Phoenix says and steps forward, showing me a bundle of ropes and fabric.

"A what?" I ask, having no clue whatsoever what this is about.

Frost snickers. "A portable throne, Princess. The palace is several hours away as the Guardian flies, and it would take us two days on foot."

"I'm not letting you carry me like a... like an air ambulance patient!"

"What?" Frost looks confused. "The Queen travels this way herself."

Now it's my turn to frown. "She doesn't fly?"

"She doesn't have wings, Wyn. She's a Goddess, not a Guardian."

"But shouldn't she be able to, I don't know, magic herself from one place to another? I mean, she's a Goddess, she must be powerful, right?"

The woman and her companions stare at me openly. Apparently, they weren't aware of how clueless I am about my mother and her world.

"Wyn, your mother is the most powerful of all the Gods. Only she herself knows what she can do. For all I know, she could grow wings, or teleport, or summon a dragon to ride on, but usually, she travels by PT. That way her subjects can see her."

"There are dragons?!"

Frost laughs, putting an arm around my shoulders. "That's so you, focussing on the least important aspect of what I'm telling you."

That earns him an elbow against his ribs. He yelps. "Yes, there are dragons. Not many, though. They keep to themselves mostly. They do send an ambassador to court once a year.

Should be soon, actually, I'm sure if you ask your mother you'll get to meet him."

"We should leave, my lady, if we want to arrive before nightfall" Ada interrupts. While I was talking to Frost, the blue Guardians have set up the PT. It's a strange contraption, but it doesn't look uncomfortable. It's a bit like a swing chair, but with safety belts and a footrest. The material looks like leather, but at the same time it's smooth and soft. I'm going to need to learn so much about this world.

Again, I'm grateful for having my Guardians. Ada doesn't look very patient, and I'd never be able to know who of the triplets is who.

The PT is actually quite comfortable. I'm not sure how much I trust it in the air, though. Yes, there is a safety strap, but who knows how much that thing will swing around. But then, it's probably safer than trying to fly myself. If I can fly. I'm going to try that later, in a warm place, where I can safely take off my shirt so I can unfold my wings. Although...

"How do they have their wings out if they're wearing clothes?" I ask no one in particular, pointing to the triplets.

"Practice," Arc shrugs, and extends his own wings, despite having put on clothes again. I walk around him, looking whether they have ripped holes into his shirt. Nope. They just... float through the fabric, or whatever you want to call it. I don't get those wings... they're not quite part of their bodies, but yet there they are, growing out of their shoulder blades, moving at their commands. Magic can be so annoyingly confusing.

"Then why did you take off your shirts earlier?"

Frost snickers. "Why not?"

I groan. Men. Why do they have to know how gorgeous they are?

Ada clears her throat. Yeah, I get it, we have to leave. The triplets take the straps holding up the PT, but with a collective growl, my guys step forward and take them. Good, I feel much safer with my Guardians. No offense to the blue ones, but mine are... well, *mine*.

There are four thick straps extending from each of the corners of the throne. My Guardians take one each and wrap it around their waists, then get in position around me, their wings extended. All of them are wearing clothes now. Pity.

"Lynx and I will fly at the front, and Fox and Phoenix will take the rear," Ada commands, and her men do what she says. I'm wondering whether she is just their leader, or whether there is more between them. It's hard to tell with her tough exterior.

"All ready?"

Everybody nods, except for me, but that doesn't seem to matter. Ada bends her knees and jumps up into the air, her wings beating strongly until she's hovering several metres above ground.

Lynx is the next one to fly up - now it's our turn. Hurray. Not sure if my stomach is going to survive this. When I was younger, I used to love going to the fair, trying out all the rides, but when I got older, I began to get queasy in most of them. Not quite to the stage where I had to throw up, but enough to feel uncomfortable. I imagine myself puking while in the PT, and decide that I cannot let that happen. I'm a Princess here, after all. I need to keep face, at least for now, until everybody discovers how unregal I really am.

"Ready?" Storm asks. I sigh and nod. Let's just pretend that this is going to be fun.

As one, they jump, just about managing to keep their wings from touching. I'm hovering in the middle, the PT swinging gently, but mostly under control. I'm really glad my feet aren't in the air but safely on the footrest. I'm looking down at the ground that is quickly becoming further and further away. The Guardians are flying fast - not quite plane-fast, but close. A cold wind is tousling my hair and biting my cheeks. I could do with a winter jacket right now. But my bags are... where are my bags? Before the battle, we left them in the car, planning to pick them up before going through the Gate. But when I saw my guys on the rainbow bridge, they weren't carrying anything. I guess the shock of me being knocked out distracted them. Oh well, I hope my mother has some warm clothing prepared for me. Yes, I'm from Scotland, but we mainly get rain and not a lot of snow, at least not in Edinburgh. I'm not used to this kind of dry cold. I shiver and wrap my arms around my chest.

"Use your magic!" Storm calls to me.

"I can't!" I shout back. it dawns on me that I haven't told them yet about my magic being blocked. I was busy with other... things. Like having sex with Storm.

Chapter Nineteen

The palace is huge. Huge like in massive. Ginormous. It's basically an entire walled city, but all in one large complex. And it looks like something Tolkien would have dreamed up. Turrets reach high into the sky, looking down on intricate walkways and large courtyards. There are gardens all over the place, but not green and colourful like you'd expect them to be. Instead, they're shades of blue and white. This is the home of the Winter Queen, after all.

Flags are waving in the wind, but I can't make out what's on them yet. Maybe it's because my eyes are teary from the cold. I miss my magic terribly. Inside of me is a big, dark hole where she used to live. The cave, still blocked, is empty and cold. It's almost painful when I focus on it.

"We'll land on the Queen's Tower!" one of the triplets shouts against the icy wind. After Storm noticed that I couldn't conjure any warm air myself, he did it for me, but I'm still cold. The wind is too strong.

We change course, circling the palace. Down below, people are going about their business, scurrying like little bees looking after their hive. There are hundreds of people outside, and I can't even begin to imagine how many more will be inside the buildings.

Around the walls of the palace, a town has grown. You can see that it wasn't planned this way; there are no straight roads or orderly houses. Instead, it's a chaotic mishmash of tiny alleys winding around buildings that look like they've been randomly placed on the ground. They're made from some kind of stone that shimmers in the last light of the day. It looks beautiful.

Out of nowhere, a face appears in the air in front of us. A massive, creepy face of a man with wild eyebrows and a Father Christmas beard. It's as tall as all four of my Guardians stacked on top of each other. Weird. Well, they told me that I'd come across some strange magic here.

We're hovering in front of the face, waiting for something. The face isn't moving, the eyes aren't even blinking. That makes it even creepier.

"What is…" I whisper to my Guardians, but the face interrupts me with a booming voice that's somehow both inside and outside of my head.

"Princess Wynter. What are you seeking at her Majesty's palace?"

Ehm, wanting to visit my mother? Heading her call? Shouldn't her… guard-face know that?

"The Princess has come at the behest of her mother, Queen Beira, Mother of Gods," Storm shouts against the rising wind.

"And can the Princess speak for herself?" the face replies, finally blinking for the first time. No, it's still creepy.

"She can!" I shout back. "I was invited, so let us in!"

Probably not the politest response, but I'm cold. Sue me.

"Her Majesty is currently unavailable. Please hold."

What. The. Fuck. Is he some kind of magic call centre operative?

Suddenly, there's another voice in my head, this one female, and rather bossy. "Bernold, what the heck are you doing? You're not supposed to... oh my, your Majesty!"

The man's face blinks out of existence, before being replaced by another one. A woman this time, with puffy cheeks, white hair and laughing lines all around her eyes and lips. She looks like a grandmother who's just caught one of her grandchildren red-handed.

"Princess, I am so sorry. Bernold must have slipped into the control room while I wasn't looking... Come on in, forgive me, he's going to be punished *severely*." The last word is dripping with poison and just before her image disappears, she turns around to look at something behind her, fury written all over her face. I almost feel sorry for Bernold, whoever he is.

The air shimmers in front of us where the giant face was just a moment ago, and without a word, Ava and her triplets begin to fly towards the palace. We follow and I lean as far I dare to out of the PT to see more of my mother's home. The closer we get to the buildings, the bigger they seem. Holyrood Palace in Edinburgh is like a shed compared to this one. I start to count the towers, but shouts below distract me. People are standing and pointing towards us. I wiggle uncomfortably on the PT.

Can they see my bum? How do I look from below? Am I going to be stared at a lot from now on?

Usually, I'm one to avoid attention. I've never fought to be in the spotlight, and even though I often took the lead in teamwork back at school and university, I prefer to work from inside the group, not as their leader. I've got a feeling this might all change now that we've finally arrived in the Realms.

We've almost reached the tallest tower of them all. It's pearl white and shimmers in the evening light. Like everything, it's got a distinct wintery feel to it all. That's not to say, everything here is snow-covered or made from ice. No, it's more the way things seem to be smooth and gleaming. The colours are all in the white and blue spectrum, with few things yellow or red. Okay, this is why I'm not an artist. I'm terrible at describing things.

Basically, it's magnificent.

A large door opens at the top of the tower, giving us a way in. I sigh as we finally fly inside and away from the staring crowds. I can't wait to get out of the PT. It's not uncomfortable, but I prefer not to be carried through the air like a baby.

Four attendants are waiting for us, standing unmoving while my Guardians help me out of my throne.

I'm a little unsteady on my feet. I'll be glad if I never have to sit on that PT again. Why can't they just use planes, or helicopters? Then it dawns on me that they may not have electricity. I look around the room. A ball of light is hovering on the ceiling where you'd usually find a lamp. It's pulsating somehow, and it's definitely got an 'alive' kind of vibe to it. Definitely not powered by electricity, but by magic. I wonder if I could create a ball like that. It's not really fire, it's more like concentrated light. I make a mental note to ask Crispin later on.

A wooden door bangs open behind the guards and the woman from the massive face thingy steps into the room. She's a little out of breath; I assume they don't have elevators here to get to the top of the towers.

She gives me a quick curtsey. "Your Royal Highness, it's a pleasure to welcome you to the palace. I'm Tamara, the Head of Household."

Frost snickers behind me, but I don't want to be impolite, so I don't turn around to find out what's so funny about that.

"Very nice to meet you," I say and smile at her. She looks friendly, but there is steel behind her eyes. She's a strong woman who shouldn't be crossed.

She huffs. "And apologies again about Bernold. He's been assigned bedpan duty in the infirmary for the next month." She winks at me. Oh, apparently she's got a sense of humour, too. I like her already. "Follow me, Princess."

I do as she says, but Storm is quicker and takes the lead. Surely he doesn't need to be this protective in my mother's palace?

The other three follow, while Ada and her Guardians stay behind.

There's a short corridor, leading to a large stone staircase. It goes down a long way; looking down the hole in the middle makes me shudder with vertigo. No wonder Tamara was out of breath; this is like climbing a mountain. Luckily we're going down now, not up.

At the sides of the stairwell are two small crystal balls mounted on pedestals, the swirling white clouds inside them reminding me of snow globes. Tamara puts a hand on one of them and it lights up brightly. There's a rumbling noise and - oh my Gods, the stair case is moving.

"Stairs or slide?" she asks, but I just look at her cluelessly.

"Slide," Frost replies in my stead, and she gives him a conspiratory smile. Surely she's not talking about a -

The steps sink down and merge together, forming a slide, gently shimmering like smooth pearls.

"Wow." I take a deep breath.

"Welcome ta the palace," Arc laughs. "Throne room?"

Tamara nods.

"Watch and learn, lass," he says, and steps onto the top of the slide. "Second floor," he commands loudly, and a red line appears on the pearl white, snaking down the slide, disappearing into the distance. With a grin, he sits down. "Fast, please."

In a flash, he's whisked away, racing down the slide at breakneck speed. Wow. That looks like fun!

"You simply state the destination and speed you'd like," Crispin explains. "There's slow, gentle, medium, fast and Queen."

"Queen?"

"Her Majesty doesn't like to be kept waiting," Tamara answers my question.

"Would you like to ride with one of us?" Crispin asks and I give him an incredulous look.

"No way!"

I sit down at the top of the slide, marvelling at how soft and warm it feels. "Second floor, medium," I say confidently. The floor vibrates slightly, and off it goes. It's not like a normal slide, where you move down on your own accord. Here, the *slide* moves and I stay in place. It's a good speed, but I regret not choosing fast. That looked like more fun. Next time.

I don't see much of the floors I pass while on the slide. It's too fast, all I can see are blurry outlines of doors. After about a minute, I finally reach the second floor where the slide comes to a halt. Behind me, I can already hear Frost cheering and whooping. Sounds like he's taken the fast option. I jump to my feet and step off the slide to make way for him. Being crushed by a Guardian isn't on my to-do list today.

Arc is waiting a few steps away from the landing, in a large and bright chamber, decorated with delicate wall hangings. There are no chairs; the only furniture is a pedestal at the front, next to a massive set of doors. A man is standing there; from his perfect features it's clear that he's a Guardian. His immaculate suit and meticulously styled beard give him the air of someone important. When he sees us approach, he steps away from his lectern and bows deeply.

"Your Royal Highness, it's an honour to finally meet you. My name is Jonathan, and I am your mother's Lord Chamberlain. I trust the journey wasn't too difficult?"

Apparently, no one has told him that there's been assassination attempts and a battle in the past few days. Well, I won't enlighten him. Maybe there's a reason Beira is keeping it to herself.

Instead, I smile sweetly. "Oh, it's been no trouble at all. Is my mother awaiting me?"

Behind me, Arc is trying to suppress a grumbling laughter. I imagine the vibrations I'd feel on his chest if I was leaning against him... No, don't think with your ovaries, think with your brain. You're a princess now, Wyn!

Jonathan scoffs. Apparently, I didn't respond royally enough. Sorry, I'm new to all this.

"Her Majesty is in a council meeting, but it should be over any minute or so. Please, do make yourselves comfortable while you wait." He makes a swooping gesture, as if he was pointing towards some non-existent chairs we could sit in.

Uncomfortably, we wait. The other Guardians have joined us, and we stand together, not quite sure what to do. Now I know why my mother hasn't put any furniture into her vestibule. It makes her guests uncomfortable and insecure - and likely more pliable in negotiations.

I square my shoulders. This shouldn't affect me. But it does. I'm having to wait here to see my mother, who is busy in some meeting. I've gone through so much to get here, and now she can't even hurry up? Does she even want to see me?

Someone grips my hand and I look up into Storm's calm eyes. "It'll be okay," he whispers, and I nod. Right. I've got my Guardians with me. Even if my mother doesn't care about me, they do.

With a creak, the doors open and we break apart. The guys take a step back, respectfully letting me go first. I'm not sure if Guardians are always this... let's call it *familiar*, with their charge. Maybe it's better if I don't show how much they mean to me? There's so much I need to learn.

Jonathan clears his throat. "Your Highness, please follow me."

I take a deep breath and do as he says, accompanying him into the throne room.

Wow.

My breath catches in my throat as I take in my surroundings. It's beautiful and intimidating at the same time. Everything sparkles and glitters in the bright light that comes from hundreds of pulsating stars floating close to the high ceiling. White marble columns carved with intricate designs lead the way to the throne. High stained-glass windows line the walls, interspersed with tapestries. There are animals and people woven into the fabric, and I make a mental note to inspect them closer later on. I'm sure they tell some kind of story.

Trying to ignore all the beautiful things around me, I turn towards the throne. It sits on a dais at the far end of the hall, accessed by crystal steps. At first, I think that the spikes emanating from the back of the throne are part of a star, but then I realise that they're actually one giant snowflake, surrounding my mother like a halo.

As always, I'm amazed at her ethereal beauty. Her long, white hair reaches her thin waist, and her eyes are as piercing as the winter she represents. She is tall and slim, but still imposing on the large throne. It was built for her, that much is obvious. It highlights her power, her shine, her majesty. Only now do I realise how powerful she really is. She's not just a queen, she's a Goddess. The mother of all Gods, they call her. Who knows if that is true. Ewww. That would mean that I've got lots of half siblings. Most of which are ancient. No, maybe it's just a figure of speech. And who knows how Gods are born. Created. Thrown into this world.

"Wynter," she says softly and gets up in one smooth motion. "It is so good to see you, my daughter."

Her voice is full of chimes and snowflakes - both warm and cold, friendly and distant. I can't get a read on her. Is this just an act?

"I am happy to see you, mother," I reply just as formally.

"My advisors have told me of your difficult journey. I'm sure you'd like to rest."

I huff. "No, actually, I would like to talk to you."

My Guardians wince behind me, but I ignore them. This is about my mother and me. We've got some talking to do. Lots of it. We've got twenty-two years to catch up on.

A muscle twitches on her cheek. "Very well, follow me. Your Guardians can go to their quarters. I've assigned them rooms close to your own."

Storm gives me a quick look, and I nod. I'll manage this on my own.

I walk towards the throne where my mother is waiting for me. She's wearing a long, flowing gown that hugs her figure. If you just looked at her body, not her face, you'd think she was in her mid-twenties. But it's her eyes that show that she's a very old soul in a young body. They are full of wisdom and knowledge, and just as much pain. And right now, they're smiling at me. Maybe she really is happy to see me.

Beira leads me through a narrow door hidden behind the throne, and along a dark corridor until we reach a small room. After all the pomp and grandiosity in the throne room, this is very different. I prefer it, though. Two large sofas face each other, and a few armchairs surround a lit fireplace built into the white stone walls. Again, there are tapestries, but these are warm and colourful, depicting animals that I don't recognise. I've never thought about what kind of wildlife they have here in the Realms, but apparently it's very different from Earth's fauna.

My mother beckons me to sit, and I take my seat on the sofa opposite. She looks a little disappointed that I didn't sit down next to her, but her expression quickly smoothens.

She snaps her fingers and suddenly a yellow light appears around the doorframe.

"Now nobody will be able to listen in," she explains with a smile. With another gesture, two wine glasses appear on a little table between us. Instead of taking one though, she looks at me. I squirm a little under her inquiring eyes.

But then she smiles, "I'm glad you requested to speak with me in private - had it come from me, people may have become suspicious."

I stare at her, not understanding what this is about. Apparently, she can see the questions on my face.

"There is a lot going on that I have not been able to explain to you, Wynter—"

"People call me Wyn," I interrupt.

She smiles again. "That's what I call you in my mind. How wonderful that I can finally address you as such in real life." Her expression turns serious again. "Not everything is as it may seem to you. There are many things we have to talk about, and I'm sure you have questions... but first, tell me, what's going on between you and those yummy Guardians?"

I gape at her, speechless. Excuse me? My mother - who's been absent for most of my life - is asking me about my... love life? And did she really just call them 'yummy'?

"Oh, don't look at me like that," she laughs. "It's obvious - even if I didn't have my sources telling me how close you have become. And I'm so happy for you - they are the best Guardians I could find."

I still don't have any words to respond. This is too surreal. Ground, please swallow me now. I need to change the topic.

"My magic is gone," I blurt out. She raises an eyebrow, knowing exactly what I'm doing. But then she turns serious as she realises what I just said.

"What happened?"

I tell her about the battle, how I did that stupid thing of trying to kill lots of demons at the same time. When I finish describing how I was trapped within my own body, she frowns.

"I will have my court physician examine you."

"Thank you, but I don't think it's anything physical. It's like my magic is trapped and I can't get her out."

"Don't worry, our physicians deal with both physical and magical emergencies," she says soothingly, but a small line has started to appear between her brows. Not as unfazed as she seems. "I had planned to talk to you further, but this shouldn't wait."

She snaps her fingers again and the yellow glow around the door disappears. My mother closes her eyes for a few seconds, then opens them again, looking straight at me with her sparkling blue eyes.

"Theodore will come to your chambers. Tamara is waiting outside to show you the way. I will join you there shortly."

She's all back to business, the earlier smile a faint echo on her lips.

I give her a short nod, not sure what to say, and leave the room.

Chapter Twenty

Istare at the girl in the mirror. She's so familiar and yet so foreign. Smooth, flawless skin, beautifully curved cheekbones, eyes surrounded by long lashes that make makeup obsolete. Her eyes are brighter than they should be.

This is supposed to be me. And until a moment ago, I hadn't even realised that I'd changed. The last time I saw myself was in Chesca's house. Before I got wings. Before the rainbow. Before Aodh died.

Someone clears their throat behind me and I turn around, ripping my gaze off the mirror. I don't want to think about looking different. I liked me being normal, ordinary. I never wanted to look like a demi-goddess. Wings, I can get used to, but those cheekbones? Nah.

"Your Highness, I am Theodore, her Majesty's physician. I've been told you've been experiencing problems with your magic?"

Yeah, you could call it a problem. A rather big one.

"Yes, ever since... I think I used too much magic at once. I blacked out, and ever since I can't access my magic."

"Do you still feel the connection to it?"

I shake my head. "I know it's still in me, but I can't reach it. She's buried in her cave and I can't get her out." I huff in frustration. Telling others about it makes me feel like a total failure. How the hell did I manage to bury my own magic?

He looks at me in confusion. "She? A cave?"

I frown. "Yes, my magic lives in a cave close to my heart. I thought it was that way for everyone?"

"Magic presents differently in each person, but a cave... and talking about magic as a person... I've not come across that before."

I shrug uncomfortably. "What does your magic look like?"

He's clearly taken aback my question and takes a moment to think. "It's a large ball of light in my chest."

I wait for more but apparently, that's it. Seriously? How boring is that!

I almost imagine my cat stretching her claws in response, but no, the boulders are still covering the entrance to her cave.

"May I examine you, Princess?"

No? "Yes, what do I need to do?"

"Just sit on the sofa; most people prefer to sit or lie down. Close your eyes, and I will feel for your magic and try and connect with it. You might feel a gentle tug, but don't respond to it for now."

That doesn't sound too bad. I do as he asks and wait for something to happen. All I notice is something pressing against my bum from below the lining of the sofa. Princess and the Pea, that's what I feel like.

Nothing is happening. At least, nothing I can feel. Maybe he's doing stuff with my magic? I resist the urge to open my eyes. Patience, Wyn, is a virtue. Well, the same could be said for impatience. In my opinion.

Finally, he clears his throat and I take that as a sign to look up at him.

"I could not reach your magic. It's like... you've never had any in the first place."

I gape at him. "I can reassure you that I have had magic. It's still in there!" I jump up, but then I don't know what to do. I feel like running out of the room. Real mature, I know.

I manage to swallow my anger somehow. It's not his fault that I feel like something has been ripped away from me, mangled, then pushed inside again, but with a new lock that I cannot open. Damn that magic. Damn me for being cocky. Damn those demons. Damn the whole wide world.

I punch the wall.

It hurts.

What a surprise.

My mother chooses this precise moment to enter my quarters.

"Wynter, whatever are you doing?!"

I look down at my bleeding hand, grimacing sheepishly. "Having an argument with the wall?"

My voice quivers, and I hope that she doesn't notice. I'm not sure I can deal with my mother's frosty response to my emotions. I remember, once, on one of her rare visits, when I fell and hurt my knee. I must have been no older than five or six. It hurt like hell and what I would have wanted is for my mother to kneel beside me, give me a hug, put a plaster on the wound... eh, scratch. Instead, she walked on, calling me to follow her, totally ignoring my pain. I was limping after her, crying, devastated by the complete lack of empathy. Back then, I didn't understand why she was so cold towards me. When we got back to my adoptive parents' home, I showed my knee to my mum and she did what I had been craving all afternoon: a long, warm hug.

Right now, I could use one of those.

Where are my Guardians when I need them?

"Leave us," my mother commands, and the physician bows, shooting us a curious glance as he steps out of the room. Good riddance.

Beira approaches me hesitantly. Gone is the commanding queen she was just a second ago. Now, she looks unsure of herself. Maybe I don't want that hug after all. I can't deal with the confusion of my mother suddenly not being icy.

But then I'm in her arms and I hug her back. She slowly starts patting me on the back, like she's not quite sure what she's doing. This is the first time I've ever been touched by her.

Her skin is cool and soft as our cheeks touch, mine wet with tears I didn't notice running down my face. She continues the back-patting and I'm tempted to tell her to stop, but at the same time, I don't want this hug to end. Who would have thought, my mother embracing me. Weird. I think I'm beginning to understand that there's more to Queen Beira than what I've seen for the past twenty-two years.

When we step away from each other, she grasps my hand and blows on it, like a mother would do for a toddler. Except that when I lift my hand to look at it, it's fully healed. A bit of dried blood is the only sign that I ever punched that stupid wall. Wow. Guess it's not just Crispin who can heal. Although she did it in a very different way; I didn't see any magic at all.

She shrugs as she sees my amazement. "I can teach you how to do that."

"Really?"

She gives me a small smile. "Your Guardians told me of the abilities you've exhibited so far. We'll have to see how closely they match what I can do, but I'm sure you'll be able to learn some of my skills."

"What can you do?" I blurt out. She laughs, a beautiful sound of icicles chiming in a frosty morning breeze.

"Too much to talk about right now. But before we can get to that, we need to fix your magic."

Oh, right. My mood falls to depression level again.

"I assume from your little wall outburst that Healer Theodore didn't have a solution?"

I nod. "He couldn't feel my magic. But I know it's still there! It's just buried, locked away. It's there but I can't reach it."

She frowns and puts a cool hand on my arm. "Mind if I take a look?"

I wonder why she didn't do that in the first place, but nod again.

"This might feel a little... overwhelming," she warns me, and a second later I know exactly what she means by that.

It's like I'm suddenly floating in space, my body gone, nothing but stars around me. It's beautiful and frightening. There's no sound, no wind, no movement at all. Nothing but darkness and stars. And me, little me, floating in a vacuum with no idea of how I got here. I try to move, but nothing happens. Guess you can't move without a body.

"Wyn, can you hear me?" a loud voice suddenly booms from all around me.

"Ehm, yes?" I ask into the nothingness around me. And notice that I can't hear my voice. It's only in my head.

"You need to stay put for just a few more minutes while I try and figure out your magic," my mother's majestic voice resonates in my head. I shudder (without a body, which is weird). Here, she really sounds like a Goddess. I turn around, looking at the stars. It's beautiful in a cold way. No nebulas, black holes, falling stars, just small, golden balls dotted around the black emptiness.

I huff and wait. As beautiful as this is, there isn't much to focus on. And I miss my body.

I begin to hum a random song, but stop when I can't hear myself sing. Not that that's a bad thing, I've been told that my singing voice is rather... well, let's just say it's enough for some drunk karaoke.

With a flash of light, I'm suddenly back in the present. Good riddance, creepy stars.

My mother's hands are hugging my cheeks and her piercing blue eyes are staring into mine. They're full of worry and seriousness. Oh no, please don't give me bad news. I much prefer happy news. Like, I'll snap my fingers and your magic will be back. That kind of stuff. Not the end-of-the-world scenario that's been playing at the back of my mind ever since I woke up from my locked-in state.

"Wyn, there's a problem with your magic," my mother begins.

I step back, away from her cold hands. "Tell me something I don't know!" I huff, my voice coming out sharper than I intended.

She doesn't react, which makes me worry even more. I draw my fingers through my hair, finding an occupation for them to stop them from fidgetting.

"When you killed all those demons, their life energy was set free. Imagine it as a mixture of your magic and your soul, your essence. Yours is bright as starlight, but theirs is dark and tainted. There was so much energy in the air that it would have been harmful to everybody standing around those demons. I think you may have instinctively absorbed some of it to protect your Guardians. I don't know how, but it's in you, a dark magic surrounding your own. And your magic was clever, she saw that the darkness would hurt you, so she barricaded herself away, imprisoning both herself and the demon energy." She sighs. "I can set her free, but that would also mean releasing the dark magic. It could kill you."

Wow. Did she just tell me that I could die? I shake my head. "There must be another way to get my magic back. You're the Mother of Gods, for fuck's sake! You must be able to do *something*!"

The door opens and a moment later, Storm's deep voice caresses my ear. "I agree." His strong arms surround me and I lean back against my Guardian's chest, drinking in his warmth. I need him. He can fix things, I'm sure of it. He's Storm, he's strong.

My mother straightens her shoulders. The Queen has returned, pushing away the concerned mother I had just witnessed for the first time.

"Watch your tone, Guardian," she warns him. "Wyn, I will ask my Council to do some research. For now, your magic will have to stay locked. Do not try to access it, no matter what."

With that, she leaves the room. Thanks a lot, *mummy*.

Storm gently grabs my shoulders and turns me until I'm looking into his eyes. There's darkness in them, and thunder, and something soft. My Storm. I stretch my toes and kiss him. It takes him a second to respond, then his mouth opens, letting me in, while his arms press me against his body, gripping me tight. I hug him back while our tongues dance in desperation. I'm drowning in him, and it feels good.

Chapter Twenty-One

Thank the Gods that my room in this palace has a large bed. Otherwise, I'd have to sleep alone, and not cuddled in the midst of my Guardians. Crispin is on one side of me, his hand hugging my chest. He's very close to my breasts, and I'm sure if he was aware of that, he'd move. I still don't know why he pulls away whenever we get close, but for now, I need to accept that he isn't as touchy-feely as the other three. I look at Storm's sleeping figure. Okay, scratch the feely bit. Touchy, yes. Earlier, our kiss culminated in a little touching. Until the healer returned and gave us a stern glance. Ooops. Apparently, it looks bad when the Queen's daughter is kissing a Guardian while he has his hands under her shirt. I must learn more about court etiquette.

Frost is snoring softly and I'm tempted to give him a slight kick. Not just to stop the snoring. I also imagine it to be quite fun. Arc is - he's looking at me. I'm not the only one who can't sleep. I sigh and slip out from under the duvet. Sleep isn't coming. Arc grins and follows me out of the room, onto the balcony. Stars are shining brightly over the dark landscape.

They look like the same ones we have on earth. Yes, I think I can make out the Big Dipper. Or something that looks like it. Maybe it's called something else here. The Big Icicle. The Big Snowflake. Big Yeti, perhaps? And yes, I get silly when I'm tired.

I feel for my magic to conjure some warm air to dispel the night's chill - and remember that there is no magic. I sigh and suppress a shiver. Maybe the balcony was a bad idea.

"Cannae sleep, Princess?" Arc whispers into my ear and hugs me from behind.

"Give the man a medal," I joke while pushing an elbow into his abs. He growls and presses me closer against his body.

"Are ye being violent? Ye know that's not what a wee Princess is supposed ta do?"

I laugh and he joins me. His chest is rubbing against me with each of his laughing breaths. I savour the touch and wish for more.

"How are ye settling in?" he asks softly when we both fall quiet again.

"I'm not sure. Everything is so... alien. It's like I've been thrown into a fairy tale, except that instead of an evil stepmother I suddenly have one that seems more caring than I expected, and four rather than one Prince Charming."

"I can be more than just charming," he whispers seductively and I have to fight hard against the impulse to turn around and kiss him. When I don't, he lowers his head and begins to nuzzle on my neck.

"I don't know why I'm here," I say, and he stops. A second later, I'm in his arms, looking up into his beautiful, moss-green eyes.

"Yer mother had a good reason to summon ye. Trust me, this is where ye belong. This is where yer needed."

"I'm not much use without my magic." I grimace, causing him to frown. One of his hands disappears from my back only to softly stroke my cheek.

"Yer magic doesn't define ya. It's only a wee thing that makes ye even more stunning than ye are already. Ye are strong, Wyn, dinnae forget that. Hell, yer the strongest person I ken."

I don't believe him. I'm just a human girl without my magic. Just a human who has been transported into a world where everybody else has superpowers. I'm lost here, and he knows it. They all know it.

"Look, ye—" He suddenly stops and takes a step forward towards the railings, taking me with him. "Did ye see that?"

"I was looking at you, you silly Scottish Guardian. What did you see?"

He puts a finger on my lips. I want to lick it. Not now, Wyn. Priorities.

"There was someone in the bushes..."

I turn around and stare into the darkness. The only light comes from the few palace windows which are still lit. There's no moon that - shit. There's no moon. How is there no moon in this place. There needs to be a moon. For the tides and all that. Moons are essential. Werewolves, tides, an excuse to go crazy a few nights each month.

"There!" And then I finally see it. A dark figure creeping through the gardens; a shadow in the night. He's heading to the Royal quarters.

"Wake the others," Storm whispers while staring into the darkness. I shake off my no-moon thoughts and tiptoe back into the bedroom.

Three tired men are looking at me. Waking is unnecessary, so I just motion for them to follow me back out onto the balcony. Storm is about to say something, but I put a finger on my lips and he shuts up. Interesting, I should do that more often.

The guys are surprisingly quiet for being so large. Before we can join Arc outside, he's running through the room. "Quick, they just broke the window to the Queen's quarters!"

Mother. Surely, that's impossible? She must have security in place; someone shouldn't just be able to walk through the gardens and enter the palace unseen.

A strange fear grips my heart. She could be in danger. She's immortal, but does that mean she can't be killed?

I race behind Arc, the rest of the guys following us. The hallways are empty; the only light comes from flickering orbs floating below the ceiling. Someone behind me claps his hands and they immediately become bright, illuminating the corridors we're running through.

A few heads peek out of open doors, but nobody tries to stop us.

Another corner, and we can finally see the large silver door that leads to my mother's apartments in the distance. Almost there. Two guards are standing in front of it, oblivious to what might happen inside.

Storm conjures a gust of wind that slams into the door, throwing it open just in time for us running into the room. It's a small, dark chamber; the vestibule where visitors wait when they want a private audience with the Queen. Ignoring the spluttering guards, we traverse the room in a few large strides and come to a halt in front of a beautifully ornate golden door. Storm grips the doorknob and tries to open it, but it doesn't budge.

"Quickly, put your hands on the wings!" he commands and pushes me forwards. There are two wings carved into the door, spread out, ready to fly. They're so lifelike that I'd love to pause and study them, but there's no time. I lay my hands on them, feeling the rough, cold surface beneath my flushed skin. Nothing happens.

"Shit, she's not added her to the list yet," Frost curses. He turns around to the guards running towards us. "Any of you got emergency privileges?" A collective shake of heads causes Storm to kick the door and Arc to let out a stream of colourful curses.

"Stand back!" Storm shouts and we all crowd against the walls as he creates a swirling fist of wild air. Throwing his arms out in front of him, he makes the fist slam against the door. It doesn't budge. Again and again he uses his air like a battering ram, but the door stays shut.

"Let me through!" a deep voice shouts and the gathering crowd gives way to a tall man in the same dark blue uniform Ada's triplet Guardians were wearing yesterday. With the added extra of a long sword hanging from his hips.

"Gwain, thank the Gods!" Storm explains. "Someone entered her Majesty's quarters and we need to get in."

"How?" Gwain is not just tall, he looks strong. Intimidating. In command. His peppered hair is cut short, framing a weathered face. A thin scar splits his left eyebrow in two. Here's someone who's seen a lot. Battle, most likely. He exudes a sense of authority that makes me want to do whatever he asks because I know he's right. Which is dangerous. He's powerful, despite his age. Or maybe, because of it.

"They sneaked through the gardens and broke a window leading to the Royal bedroom, Sir," Storm reports. Wow, this is the first time I've heard him call anyone Sir. This Gwain guy must be important.

"Stand aside," Gwain commands and without hesitation, everybody does. He puts his hands on the door, just like I did earlier. Except that for him, the door opens with a click. Sword drawn, he enters the dark room, and we follow. Storm and Arc have pushed past me to lead the way, and I'm flanked by my other two Guardians.

It's too quiet. Something isn't right.

"Your Majesty?" Gwain calls out, but nobody replies.

"Lights," Arc whispers softly and a large icy orb above us springs into life, flooding the room with cold, bright light. My mother is lying on her bed. There's a knife in her heart.

I scream.

"Search the rooms! Luke, gather men to comb the gardens," Gwain commands. "Ado, get Theodore here right now."

While a flurry of activity happens behind us, I approach the bed where my mother lies, motionless.

"Beira?" I whisper, while Crispin runs to her other side, waving his hands over her in a complicated pattern.

"She's still alive, but barely," he says tonelessly, leading to gasps all around us. "I'm trying to stabilise her, but we need to remove that knife before it can do any further harm."

"Shall I do it?" I ask, desperate to do something.

"No, I need Theodore. It's a Summer knife, it needs to be handled by a trained healer."

"So we just sit here and wait?" I shout, fear and anger cursing through me. I point at the guards swarming the room. "How could you let this happen? Where were you all? How could someone just come in here and stab Bei... my mother?"

Someone wraps around me from behind. Salty, fresh air fills my nostrils. Frost. I shake of his arms. I don't want his touch right now. All I want is my mother to wake up. Yes, she's been absent for most of my life, but she's my mother, and she's so close to telling me all I want to know. All I need to know. I need her. She's the queen, and my mother. She's supposed to be a God, how can she lie here like that, dying?

"Where is Theodore?" Crispin shouts. "She's fading!"

"How is this knife able to kill her?" I ask, my voice breaking.

"It's a Summer knife," Crispin grinds through gritted teeth. "Forged by the King of Summer himself. Only he can harm our Queen. It's spreading his filthy essence through her body, destroying her magic, her spirit. But if we can't pull it out, we need to siphon its energy back into the knife first. Otherwise it'll just continue its destruction."

Damn. Who the hell is that summer king?

"Sir, Theodore isn't in the palace, he was called to one of the villages," a guard reports, panting heavily.

The healer isn't coming. We need to do something. My mother's face is ashen, with a slightly blue tint to her cheeks. Her hair is no longer smooth and silky, but brittle and weak. She's withering in front of our eyes and there's nothing I can do. If only my magic was here. My magic. Beira said it was holed up because of the demon energy. So if I managed to get rid of the demon energy, my magic would be free. Ready to save my mother.

A commotion outside the door makes us all turn around. A man in a blue uniform enters, followed by two guards holding a man dressed in black. He's only half conscious, his head lolling from side to side.

"Sir, we caught him not far from the Gate to the Summer Realm," the blue-clad man reports.

Gwain is by the man's side in two long strides and grab's the assassin's chin, lifting his head up until they're staring into each other's eyes.

"Any last words?" Gwain grumbles, his body poised to strike. He's going to break the guy's neck, I'm sure of it. There's no need for an interrogation, the knife says it all.

The knife.

"Stop!" I shout and everybody turns to me, startled. I hope I have this right. Otherwise this might end badly.

"What are ye doing?" Arc whispers but I shake my head. No distractions.

"Hold him tight," I command, surprised at the authority in my voice. The guards securing the prisoner give me a sharp nod and tighten their grip. Wow, apparently they really do see me as their princess.

Please work, I whisper to myself as I close my eyes and delve down into my body, searching for my magic. The cave is still there, the boulders still barring the entrance. Now that I know for sure that my magic is remaining locked inside, guarding an evil demon force, I feel even worse for her. Not only is she alone, she's also fighting a solitary battle. Not anymore.

"Oi!" I call out to her, hoping she'll hear me through the wall of stone. "I need you!"

I can almost imagine her laughing bitterly. She knows she can't get out without the dark magic escaping. But that's what I'm counting on.

"Don't be scared, we'll be able to release that demon energy!" I shout. "But I need you now, my mother is dying. Come out, help me!"

A low rumble makes me perk up. Is it working?

"Please, magic! Please!" I'm begging her. If my Guardians could see me now, shouting at a stone wall. But I know she's in there.

And finally, a rock falls to the ground. Granted, it's a tiny one, more like a pebble, but it's a start. More rocks follow, pushed off the top of the boulder wall by an unseen force. My magic is fighting. Good.

Finally, there's a hole large enough to let me in - or my magic out.

A meow is all the warning I get, then she's jumping through the air, claws barred, fur ruffled. She's followed by a blob. That's the only word that fits. A black, gooey mass that shifts its shape faster than I can see. I almost dry heave at its sight. It's like someone has distilled nightmares, then mixed it up with despair and a good sprinkling of evil. And it's hunting my magic.

I stretch out my arms and catch her just as she nears the ground. Her claws scratch my arms, but I don't care. I've got her back. My magic. In my arms. Aww.

We run, closely followed by the blob. It's hurting my insides as it pursues us through my body. We need to get to the surface before it catches up with us. I need to get it outside.

My magic whimpers, but there's no time to soothe, no time to reassure her.

"I need your power," I pant while running. "I need to get that thing out of me and into the vessel." I'm trying not to think of the 'vessel' as a living, breathing man. He tried to kill my mother. He made his choice. He's earned his fate.

With a soft meow, my magic gives her permission. Power floods me, curses through me with an intensity I've not felt before. Maybe this is what an addict feels getting their first fix after going cold turkey for a while.

I open my eyes. Everything is brighter, more vibrant than before. I can see magic again, swirling around the people in the room. They are all Guardians; they all have their own kinds of magic. And in their midst, the assassin. The guards are still holding him tight, ignoring his weak struggles.

I feel the blob burning through my insides. My knees are going weak. It's time.

I reach out and grab it, fighting to keep it in my grasp. It's slippery and burns as I touch it, and I can't help but scream as

I try to pull it out of me. It's holding on, grasping for halt as I squeeze it tightly. Damn, that thing is strong.

I pour all my energy into my grip on it, willing it to stop fighting. No such luck. It's thrashing and firing burning missiles at me. As my vision goes and I can feel my body sink to the floor, something new enters me. A new energy. No, four. Four strands of cooling magic join my own, wrapping themselves around the blob. Finally, its struggle is getting weaker. Pushing against its resistance, I draw the dark energy out of myself and into the open. I can feel myself losing consciousness; I need to be quick. I push the blob towards the struggling man, careful to keep it contained. I don't even want to know what it could do if it was to be set free. Only a tiny bit further... I stuff the blob into the assassin's mouth and into his centre. He fights me, but he's too weak. The blob wants to stay there, it's no longer trying to resist. It wants a new host, and it doesn't care who that is.

Finally, I release my grip on it and retreat. As soon as I let go, a wave of energy pushes into me, giving me the strength to open my eyes again. The man's face has turned grey, his eyes black. Dark veins are appearing on his skin, making him look something like a zombie.

"Kill him," I whisper to the guards, assuming that they will carry out my command. Sitting up, I turn around, towards my mother. This isn't over yet.

"Help me up," I say to no one in particular, and someone's arms lift me gently until I'm standing on my own two feet. Well, almost. I'd be back on the ground if they didn't still support me.

My mother is looking even worse. Her face has aged, her cheeks are bony, her forehead full of wrinkles that haven't been there before. Earlier today, she looked not much older than me. Now, she's aging quickly. I don't want to look. This is not the perfect, unchanging mother I've known all my life.

I sink onto the bed next to her frail body, and place my hands on her chest.

"Are you sure you can do this?" Crispin asks softly. I look into his beautiful blue eyes and wordlessly, he nods. He's seen my determination. We're going to do this.

"Use your hands to pull out the knife, while siphoning its magic into it at the same time. All of the summer magic needs to be inside the knife by the time it leaves her body. I'm going to keep her stabilised at the same time." He looks to someone behind me. "Arc, she'll need your powers."

I don't question why it has to be Arc and not one of the twins, but accept that Crispin knows his stuff.

Let's do this.

Taking a deep breath, I close my eyes again and focus on my magic. She's in her cave, sleeping from exhaustion - the cave is still partly blocked, but the entrance is large enough to let me in. I kneel by her side and gently stroke her fur.

"I need you one more time, little one. Then you can sleep," I whisper, scratching her between her ears. As she wakes, she gives me an indignant scowl. "Sorry," I mumble, but then I remember that I have a very valid reason for demanding more of her. It's my mother, after all.

I take my magic out of the cave and put her on the floor. She stretches before finally giving me access to her energy.

Okay, let's just pretend this is going to be easy. I extend my senses until I can feel the knife in my mother's body. It's a pulsating, ugly wound that is seeping black stuff into her while at the same time drawing out her life force. Like a mosquito that takes your blood while injecting something back that makes you itchy. But in this case, it's deadly.

I follow the black matter through my mother's body. It's everywhere. It's not yet reached all the cells, but it's flooding her veins and has surrounded her heart. It won't beat much longer. How the hell am I supposed to get rid of this stuff?

I decide to go back to its source: the knife. Maybe I can use it as a sort of anchor. I grip the knife tightly with my magic and begin to pull. My hands are still on my mother's chest, so the knife will stay in position - it's only the magic I'm working on right now.

Like sucking on a straw, I'm drawing the black magic out of her body. It's a slow process, and a sickening one. With every pull, I feel a tiny bit seeping into me. My magic is moving around frantically, trying to wade off the invading force, but I ignore her for now. It's not much more.

When I can no longer find black magic to suck out, I finally move my hands to grip the knife. It's cold and burning hot at the same time. I can feel blisters forming on my skin and I'm tempted to let go of it, but I can't. I have to do this. This will be worth the pain. I hope.

Steeling my mind and my body, I pull, holding the magic tight, not letting it flow out of the knife again. Then I remember I should have probably told Crispin before I started. I don't have the energy to speak, so I pull on the bond linking me to him. I know it'll be uncomfortable for him, but he'll understand. Hopefully.

The dark magic is struggling against my grip, and now that I not only have to control my magic, but also my muscles holding the knife, I'm struggling. I spent too much energy earlier; there's almost none left. And at the same time, I feel some of the knife's magic seep into me. I'm pretty sure I'm going to regret this whole thing. I mean, that's what got me into this mess, overestimating my powers.

Then, the knife is out. I'm shaking all over, and it falls onto the bed, narrowly missing my mother. I hope Crispin is looking after her, because I can't.

I let myself fall, sinking into unconsciousness.

"Wyn," someone whispers. "Time to get up, little Princess."

I wince. It's too loud, despite the whispering. Do they have sledgehammers in the Realms? Because that's what it feels like. Ouch. My head.

"Let her sleep," another voice says, not even trying to be quiet. I want to kill them, slowly. But that would be too much work, I'd actually have to open my eyes. No, better go back to sleep. I was dreaming of something nice, something involving lots of limbs and... other body parts.

"But I'm bored," the first voice whines. Oh, well. They asked for it. I reach for my magic and pull a few strands out, wrapping them around my target.

"What's wron—", I don't let the other one finish and give them the same magic treatment. There, now I can sleep.

"Wyn, wake up. You need to release your magic from these idiots. The Commander wants to talk to them and they can't speak."

I stretch, waking from a restful sleep. It takes me a moment to remember. Oh yes, I took their voices. Crispin and Arc. Not my fault, they didn't let me sleep.

I open my eyes and smile at the Guardians sitting around my bed. They stare at me.

"What's up boys?" I ask cheerily, but the effect is somewhat ruined by my hoarse voice. Frost conjures some water into the empty glass next to me and I drink it greedily.

Arc gets up, gesticulating wildly. I pretend not to understand him.

"Crispin, would you mind telling me what he's trying to say?" My voice is sweet as honey. Frost is holding onto his chair, fighting to suppress his laugh, and even Storm is trying to hide a smile.

Crispin gives me the finger. Yes. Crispin. The sweet healer. Gives. Me. The. Finger. He's never going to speak again.

"Princess, we need to get going," Storm chuckles. "We stayed as long as we could, but the Commander wants a report. Crispin says your vitals are back to normal, and—"

"Crispin *says*?" I interrupt, causing Frost to fall into another laughing fit.

"He wrote it down, actually," Storm explains, his mask slowly taking over his face again. Damn, I like it when he smiles. " I didn't think I'd ever ask this, but please let them talk again."

I sigh dramatically and remove the magic around Arc's vocal chords. In response, he starts humming. Yes, why not. I ignore him and turn to Crispin, who's looking at me stone-faced. He's pissed, no doubt about that.

"What do I get for letting you speak again?"

He doesn't reply but I didn't expect him to.

"A kiss, perhaps?"

I know that's evil of me. But I need to feel his lips on mine or this bond is going to drive me crazy. It's become a lot less aggravating with the other three since... the rainbow, but with Crispin, I still want to rip his clothes off whenever I see him. Maybe a kiss will make it better.

He looks at me, his eyes blue and sad. Then he walks out of the room, leaving me in shock. What have I done! This wasn't right. Ashamed, I remove the magic binding his voice, and curl up in bed.

Epilogue
Beira

She's grown up so much since last I saw her. She's no longer the skinny little girl trying to show me her world. Now she's a woman and I've brought her into my own. But is she ready for what I will ask of her?

Wyn is sitting on a chair by my bed, looking uncomfortable. She still doesn't know what to think of me. I don't blame her. I've treated her like a stranger for all her life. I wish she knew that it was all just an act. That I didn't have a choice to give her away, to stay distant, to not show my true feelings. That I always had people watching her, making sure she was safe.

But she saved me, and that must mean that all is not lost between us. Maybe with time, we could become closer, like a real mother and daughter. But time is something that we don't have.

This wasn't the first assassin Angus sent, nor will it be the last. It's what I expect him to do it, it's in our nature. He's the Summer King, I'm the Winter Queen. He's the Father of Gods, and I am the mother. But now that he's tried to kill my daughter, he's gone too far. The attack on the ferry was clearly him, and so was the kidnapping before. But not the demons. I don't know why there were demons, and that scares me. Even Angus wouldn't steep so low.

I'm not sure how much to tell Wyn. She doesn't know anything about this world, and it's my fault. At least she's got her Guardians. That's one thing I did right, at least. They will keep her safe when I'm no longer here.

Because my time is running out.

*Continue Wyn's story in **Winter Heiress**.*
The entire Daughter of Winter series is also available as a box set and as audio books.

*And if you're interested in what happened to Chesca after Aodh's death, read her story in Demon's Revenge - download it for free: **https://BookHip.com/RJXLJQD***

*Or if you want to know more about Wyn's parents, take a look at the prequel to this series, **Mother of Gods**.*

If you enjoyed this book, please consider leaving a review.

About the Author

Skye MacKinnon is a USA Today & International Bestselling Author whose books are filled with strong heroines who don't have to choose.

She embraces her Scottishness with fantastical Scottish settings and a dash of mythology, no matter if she's writing about Celtic gods, cat shifters, or the streets of Edinburgh.

When she's not typing away at her favourite cafe, Skye loves dried mango, as much exotic tea as she can squeeze into her cupboards, and being covered in pet hair by her tiny demonic cat.

Subscribe to her newsletter:
skyemackinnon.com/newsletter

facebook.com/skyemackinnonauthor

twitter.com/skye_mackinnon

instagram.com/skyemackinnonauthor

bookbub.com/authors/skye-mackinnon

goodreads.com/SkyeMacKinnon

Also By

Find all of Skye's books on her website, skyemackinnon.com, where you can also order signed paperbacks. Many of her books are also available as audiobooks.

Claiming Her Bears (Post-apocalyptic bear shifter RH)

Rescued by Bears

Protected by Bears

Craved by Bears

>> Box set

Infernal Descent (paranormal RH based on Dante's Inferno, co-written with Bea Paige)

Hell's Calling

Hell's Weeping

Hell's Burning

>> Box set

Seven Wardens (Paranormal RH co-written with Laura Greenwood)

From the Deeps

Into the Mists

Beneath the Earth

Within the Flames

Above the Waves

Under the Ice

Rule the Dark

Prequel: Beyond the Loch

Spin-off: Through the Storms

>> Box set (books 1-4)

>> Box set (books 5-7)

The Lost Siren (post-apocalyptic, paranormal RH co-written with Liza Street)

Song of Blood

Lullaby of Death

Melody of Souls

Starlight Highlanders Mail Order Brides (m/f alien romance, part of the Intergalactic Dating Agency)

Thorrn

Eron

Cyle

Between Rebels (sci-fi RH set in the Planet Athion shared world)

Stolen By Them

Guarded By Them

Chosen By Them

>> Box Set

The Intergalactic Guide to Humans (sci-fi romance, RH, m/f and fmf)

Alien Abduction for Beginners

Alien Abduction for Professionals

Alien Abduction for Experts

Alien Abduction for Pirates

Alien Abduction for Santa

The Mars Diaries (Sci-fi RH linked to the Claiming Her Bears series)

Alone

Hidden

Found

>> Box Set

Through the Gates (dystopian RH co-written with Rebecca Royce)

Purgatory City

Defiance (contemporary dark RH)

Frozen Heart

Loving Heart

Broken Spirit

Stolen Soul

Academy of Time (time travel academy standalones)

Taking Her Vikings

Exploring Her Professor

Saving His Queen

Catnip Assassins (urban fantasy reverse harem)

Meow

Scratch

Purrr

Hisss

Lick

Claw

Roar

Thud (Christmas special)

\>> Box set Books 1-4

\>> Box set Books 5-7

\>> Box set Books 1-7

Aliens and Animals (sci-fi romance co-written with Arizona Tape)

The Alien's Zookeeper

The Alien's Veterinarian

Daughter of Winter Series (Paranormal reverse harem)

Winter Princess

Winter Heiress

Winter Queen

Winter Goddess

\>> Box set

Mother of Gods (prequel)

Demon's Revenge (spin-off)

Samhain Goddess (sequel)

Standalones

Song of Souls – fairy tale retelling

Cupid's Apprentice - paranormal RH

Storm Witch - historical paranormal RH

Their Hybrid – steampunk RH

Partridge in the P.E.A.R. - sci-fi RH co-written with Arizona Tape

Highland Butterflies – lesbian romance

Anthologies and Box Sets

Hungry for More – charity cookbook

Daggers & Destiny – a Skye MacKinnon starter library

Printed in Great Britain
by Amazon

27094893R00166